The Chaplain: Sacrifice for Love

LYNN HAMMOND

DISCLAIMER

This book contains references to rape, PTSD, anxiety attacks, and some mutilation. If any of these subjects are likely to trigger an unwanted reaction, it may be best to avoid this book. If you choose to continue reading, know that this is a story of growth, love, and healing, and is in no way meant to glorify any form of abuse.

1

Sophia

"SHE'S CODING; I need the AED. Now!" A male voice hollers out…

"Beep! Beep!" What is that noise?

I'm trying to open my eyes, but they're so heavy. My body is being lifted and, now, placed on something cool. *OUCH!* I feel a shock on my chest, spreading throughout my body. I am freezing and in pain. *Why am I so cold?*

Where am I?

Another male voice speaks, "Dr. Whitest, and back. Everyone stand back."

I feel another shock. The pain radiates through my chest to my back. I let out a big gasp of air. My heart is racing. I try to move, but something is laying across my thighs.

"Quick, operating room. Now. Call down; have

her prepared for surgery. She is…not going to die on my watch," another voice says.

I feel myself being lifted again then placed on something soft. A hand pulls back my head and places some kind of object down my throat. It makes me gag.

I try, once more, to open my eyes, but they're too heavy. I want to know what is going on. Something is being laid across my body then tighten.

Hello? I want to know what is going on here. Why can't you let me up?

"All right, team, I've tightened the straps on the bed, and we're bringing her to the OR. Let's make sure we don't collide or hit anything on the way. Got it?"

I can hear so many different voices around me. The pain is really bad; I feel like someone is stabbing me in my stomach.

"Oh my god, my baby! Sophia, Sophia, can you hear me?"

That's my mother's voice.

"Ma'am, you need to move out of our way."

"Callie," a male voice appears near me. "Take Mrs. Rhinehart to the OR waiting room. We'll keep you updated."

Okay, I am a little worried now. I can hear the panic in my mom's voice. All I remember is sitting on the couch with Brad and watching *Scream*.

I remember dozing off and waking up to a crashing sound coming from my bathroom. I got up and hollered for Brad, but he never answered me back.

THE DRILLING PAIN in my head wakes me up. My body feels like someone ran over me. I open my eyes slightly. *Finally.* My head is pounding. I reach up to touch it, but a hand grabs my arm and brings it back down.

"Hey, honey!" my mother says, leaning over and in my field of vision.

Her face is blurry, and when I try to look around, all I see are black spots. I reach up and touch her cheek.

"Mom, what happened?" I say quietly.

I try to shift around so I can see her, but a violent stabbing pain hits my abdomen again. I start shaking and shivering. I can hear my heartbeat in my ears.

"Sweetie, why don't you try to rest. We are at the hospital, and the doctor told me to buzz him when you wake up." She reaches over my bed to hit the red button.

Why would I be in a hospital? I remember Brad got up to use the restroom, and I lay down on the couch, covering myself up in a blanket because he likes to turn the air down to sixty-nine degrees. When I heard the crash, I jumped up, startled, and ran to my room. I pushed open my door, and found him leaning over something in his hand. As I moved closer to him, he turned around, fast.

"Can I help you?" A woman's voice beside my head brings me back to reality and causes pain to radiate down to my temple.

I reach up to try to lower the volume, and when I do, a jolt of pain shoots down my abdomen and to my legs. The pain is increasing, and the nurse pulls out a syringe and injects it into my IV. I feel the coldness running up my arm. My heart rate increases, and I feel a tightness in my chest.

"What the hell is that?" I ask in a frog-like voice, trying to battle the panic closing in on me.

"Ma'am, this is pain medicine and a sedative. We need to get your blood pressure down and your heart rate under control. You have gone through several surgeries tonight, and we need you to stay rested for now."

All right, now I am really confused. I was just at home, enjoying a nice relaxing time with my fiancé.

The noise in the room starts fading away, and my mom is squeezing my hand, telling me it's okay and I can rest because she'll be right here.

I feel my mom's fingers rub my scalp while she sings a lullaby to me. Too weak to fight, I let myself drift asleep.

✧   ✧   ✧

"HEY! WHOSE GUN is that?" I ask Brad as I walk over to see the object in his hand.

I stop halfway across the room because he turns the gun in my direction. I just stand there, in shock, because my boyfriend of five years is pointing a gun at me.

He walks over to me, the barrel still staring me in the face, and I am backing up. I turn to run, and he hits me in the head with the gun.

For an instant, I wonder why he would do this. He just told me, tonight, how happy he was. We've finally chosen a date for our wedding.

An unsettling feeling begins to well up inside me. The look on Brad's face is not loving at all. His eyes are wide open, and his mouth is narrowed. I notice his nose is flaring. The veins in his neck are protruding. I have never seen him like this.

As the world turns black around me, the last words I hear him say are, "Tonight you die, bitch."

2

Linkin

As I arrive at the Mercy South hospital in Charlotte, North Carolina, I walk towards the admission's desk to find what room my patient is in. Sophia's mother called the church to request someone to come pray for her daughter. I was told a little about what happened to the woman, and it's a miracle she lived.

"Excuse me, I'm Chaplain Garland. Can you tell me what room Sophia Rhinehart is in?" I ask the woman behind the reception desk.

"Sure, let me pull it up," she says, clicking on her computer. "She is in room four-oh-four. If you take the elevators to the second floor and take a right, her room will be on the left."

I thank the receptionist and head toward the elevators. I walk inside and push number four on the keypad. I lean back against the wall, reflecting back to the discussion I had with the client's mother.

Hello, Reverend Garland, this is Sophia Rhinehart's mother. I was told to contact you. My daughter is in the hospital, in a coma. Her boyfriend of five years raped and stabbed her, multiple times.

Ding

The elevator stops. I step off and head toward the right. The door is cracked open, and I can hear the doctor talking.

After a few minutes, I knock.

"Come in." I recognize Sophia's mother's soft, ladylike voice.

I open the door more and stick my head in. "Good afternoon. I am Chaplain Garland." I make my way farther in the room.

"Mrs. Rhinehart, your daughter is going to need to stay in a comma for a while to let her body heal," I hear a man in a white jacket announce. "I didn't want to take this route, but due to the extensive amount of damage that has been done to her body, forced rest is safer, in order to avoid any additional stress to the tissues. She has over one thousand stitches from her upper abdomen all the way around mid-back. Her spleen was removed, and her large intestines was lacerated during the stabbing. The uterus has been attached back with multiple stitches, and I had to reconnect the anus. Your daughter has a long road ahead of her, but we're trying to put all the chances on her side."

I shudder at what this poor girl has suffered.

"Thank you, Dr. Moore," Mrs. Rhinehart says, shaking his hand.

I look around the room, and it's filled with different machines. There are four bags of solution, hanging from the IV pole. The blood pressure cuff is tightening up on her arm. Her pulse shows one hundred, and the heart rhythm looks to be normal. I hear different sounds going off.

I move closer to look at her bruised face. She has a nasal cannula in her nose, and the tubing is wrapped around her ears. I notice some blue and black spots around her neck as well.

That ass should be buried six feet under with his dick cut off, I can't help but think.

This is my first time coming to pray over someone who is not military. This fragile beaten up woman needs all the prayers she can get.

"Thank you, Reverend, for coming," Mrs. Rhinehart says, crying. "She was awake for a few minutes, but her heart rate and blood pressure spiked up because of her pain. The doctor decided to place her in a mild coma for a few days."

Just looking at how down her mother looks breaks

my heart. Her face is red and blotchy. The skin under her nose is chapped from constantly blowing her nose if I had to guess.

I reach over and place my hand on Sophia's arm and close my eyes. Her skin is warm but a little damp. I feel a nodule under my fingers. I slowly take a peek under my hand, and it's black and blue with a little blood on it. *God. This man's going to pay. That is a promise.*

I close my eyes and bow my head. "Our Father, I am here with Sophia, and she needs our prayers. I pray for healing, and for you to give her strength through the pain she will have to face, the frustration, and while her faith will be tested. She's going to need you more than ever when she wakes up and while her body heals. Be with her, Lord, in her time of need and, when she starts to feel loneliness and fear, find a way to let her know she is not alone. We make this prayer in your name, Lord. Amen." I open my eyes and see her mother has laid her head on her daughter's chest.

I back away and let her have a moment. I don't know why, but when I touched Sophia, I got a tingling sensation. Maybe because I am used to dealing with hardened military patients, not a frail, innocent woman. I can't wrap my mind around how someone can do this to the one they claim to love.

If she were mine, I would treat her like a princess.

Okay, I don't know where that came from. I shake my head to clear my mind.

As I bring my thoughts out of trouble, Mrs. Rhinehart speaks, "Reverend Garland, thank you for that sweet prayer. When she wakes up and finds out what happened she is going to be furious. The damage that S.O.B did to her is unfixable. She was so beautiful, and look at all her scars." She is walking around the bed towards me.

I'm more worried about her inside scars, the ones not seen. This beautiful woman is going to wake up scared and wonder why she deserved this.

"I am so blown away that he could do something like this. She met him when she was twenty-five, at a family reunion. He appeared at the wedding with her third cousin, Anna. When Anna brought him over to introduce us, he winked at Sophia.

"Now, as a mother, I got a little upset, but when he asked her to dance, I was convinced that he fell in love with her that day. He'd just got back from Iraq and met Anna while waiting on a taxi. She talked him into coming to the gathering to be her date. But when he left, he made sure he got Sophia's number. Those two have been together since." Her mother takes a shaky breath.

She walks over to her purse, pulls out a card, and hands it to me, The card shows a cartoon woman wearing a yellow summer dress with a sunflower in her hair. The back of the card has contact information on it. Sophia's Exotic Boutique.

Mrs. Rhinehart walks back over to Sophia's bedside. "The doctor told me, today, she will be in the hospital for about a month, then she will be discharged and head to rehab to work on building her strength. Once her body is able to stand at ninety degrees, she will be able to come home. I was told by the psychiatrist here in the hospital that she is going to need a good psychiatrist and a counselor to follow her."

"Ma'am, I am a chaplain for military families and friends. I don't understand where I fit in on helping your daughter," I say, confused. I really don't see what my profession can do for Sophia.

"Reverend. My daughter almost died. I need someone who is going to push her to get better, and I have a plan."

The way she just said that has me thinking I'm part of that plan. I stand there, waiting to hear how I can help her daughter and what her Boutique has to do with my work.

"I want you to fake your own wedding."

Fake my own wedding?

"Once she's back on her feet and able to work, I want you to pretend you need her help for the whole wedding party attire. I will pay for all expenses without Sophia knowing." She continues to explain her plan with a soft small smile.

Am I on Punk the movie. Is the woman for real?

"Let me get this straight. I'm trying not to sound like an ass here. You are trying to pay a Chaplain to lie to your daughter in order to help her get back in the swing of things?" When she nods, I continue, "Mrs. Rinehart, I don't mean anything by this, but my job is to counsel soldiers and family members that have been through a traumatic event in their life. Sophia needs a preacher she can trust, someone from her home town perhaps. Not to mention that you want me to lie to her, myself, and to God, that I'm getting married." *This woman has fallen off her rocker.*

"I know you are a military chaplain," she whispers, and her lips start to tremble. "I have heard great things about you. Sophia might not be in the army, but her attacker was. Do you know he is saying it was a trigger? Look at my daughter, Chaplain. Does it look like he just had an episode and did this to her? I am begging you to help my daughter. God will understand. You were placed here on earth to help everyone, even my precious daughter."

God, I hope I'm doing the right thing.

I look at Sophia lying quietly on the bed. My heart

flutters with anticipation for this beautiful woman. I stare at her, wondering why I am so drawn to her. I never thought someone I just met would give me so many emotions. I feel an uneasiness in my stomach. This can be dangerous and make me weak.

As my eyes scan her face, I have made my choice. I will help her, but my goal is to counsel her. I will teach her how to express her nightmares, memories, and feelings about her trauma. I don't think the approach her mother wants me to take is the right way to present it. I can see it backfiring, but I find myself accepting anyway.

"Okay," I say. "I will help you, but on one condition. Use the money you want to give me for good. Give it to a charity. I will not accept any money to help your daughter."

Now, where am I going to find a fake fiancée?

Mrs. Rhinehart swallows me into a big hug. When I try to pull away, her grip tightens. I reach around and return her hug. She lets go of me, and I step back. My stomach twists in knots with concern at what will happen when Sophia finds out the truth.

"Well, I need to head out now. I need to help back at the office," I say with a sad smile. "Contact me when you need me."

"Thank you again, Reverend. I will be in touch." Her eyes are glistening with tears.

I take a deep breath, turn, and walk out of the room. I make it back to the truck and hit the side door with my fist. Why would I say yes to this? I open the door and step up into the seat. I grab the steering wheel with both hands and lean my forehead down. *Yep, I'm in for it. I know she is going to stir up emotions that I have hidden for a long time.*

"Hear me, oh Lord, heal Sophia. Save her, and she will be saved, for you are the one I praise. Amen. Oh, and please, go ahead and forgive me now for what I'm about to do."

3

Sophia

IT HAS BEEN three months since I was brought to the hospital, and I am staring across the table at my psychiatrist. He is very skinny, and I have noticed he likes to wear tight gray suits. He has too many creases in his forehead, and his jet-black hair is combed over to one side. If I had to guess, he's hiding a bald spot. He looks like Pee-Wee Herman. He sits in his chair, patiently tapping his finger on the desk, waiting for me to express my feelings.

"Sophia, I asked you to write in your journal, just a sentence each day, describing something you did, thought, or just ate. I need you to start expressing yourself and not hold it in," he says, clicking away.

I nod, but I'm not just going to blurt out my feelings. This man is getting on my nerves. I want to just get up and slap him and call it a day. I have tried to explain that I need more time. I just went through something tragic that I almost died from. I don't get the feeling he understands what that's like.

"Okay, I'm going to ask you a simple question first. How are your bowel and bladder functioning?" he asks.

I burst out in a loud laugh. Is this some kind of joke question?

"Well, Dr. Harmon, since the day my boyfriend took a knife and stabbed me over a hundred times then decided that was not good enough and sliced me from my belly button all the way down to my anus to the point where my intestines were hanging out of my body, my shit is like diarrhea from all the scar tissue and cutting out some of the small intestines because they were already dead." I glare at him. Is this what he wants to hear?

"Good. That's good; let it out. So, tell me how you feel about this?" He scribbles something down in this black book beside him.

"If there was some way for me to kill the son-of-a-bitch I would. I would take the same knife and cut off his dick then stuff it in his mouth to eat," I say with a smirk, enjoying the idea of making this supposed therapist uncomfortable.

"Why do you want to cut his penis off for punishment?" he asks, unperturbed.

I am about to lose it now. I get up, walk over to his desk, and lean my body over so my face is close to his.

I know what he is doing. He is succeeding on getting me riled up. "He pistol-whooped me in the face," I say, my hands tightly gripping the edge of the desk. "After I fell on the ground, unconscious, he decided to have sex with me before cutting me to pieces. Does that help you understand?"

"Okay, that's enough for today, Sophia," he says, clearing his throat. "I know this was hard, but it is good for you to release some of this anger you have built up. The rage you have inside needs to be released. This man destroyed the loving, caring, and sweet girl you were. If you want to really punish him, you have to walk in with your head held high when he sees you in the courtroom." He looks straight into my eyes, making his words sink in.

He is making a little more sense now.

I AM NOW in the car, heading home. Well, it is not my home but my mother's. Until I get a bill of health from all medical doctors, I have to stay with her. The psychiatrist sent the physicians a note telling them I am suicidal and cannot be left alone. Just because I don't want to talk about my feelings doesn't make me suicidal. But, somehow, Pee-Wee's look-alike has everyone thinking I have to be cleared by him before being left alone.

No one knows that, the first night home, I went upstairs to my old room. I looked at myself in the full-length mirror, lifting my dress to see, for the first time, my scars. I used my finger and traced the scar from my bellybutton to my right hip and down my inner thigh. I placed my hand back on my bellybutton and followed the scar all the way down to my mons. I attempted to lift my leg to see the other scar that went down my vagina to my anus, but it was too painful to go near that.

I went to the bathroom and turned on the water in my tub. I had decided, when I took the blade from the hospital, that I would finish what he'd started. I turned my radio on, put on some music, and placed it beside the tub. I grabbed my hospital bag and grabbed the blade.

An hour later, the water was ice cold as I reached over for the blade that was laying on the soap dish. I pulled the safety top down and slid the razor up. I placed it on my carotid artery, pushing down lightly, and closed my eyes.

My mom came and knocked on the door. "Honey, are you okay in there? Do you need me to help you?"

I took the blade off my neck and slipped up the safety. "Mom, I am okay. I'm getting out now."

Standing up on wobbly legs, I saw my reflection in

the mirror. A little puncture hole showed on my neck, but nothing to worry about. I went to the first-aid kit underneath the sink and placed a small band aid there.

I reached out to touch the mirror, staring at my complexion, and made a promise to myself that, from that day forward, I was going to fight.

Thinking back to that day, I didn't imagine I would have come this far even if I still have so much farther to go.

THE NEXT EVENING, as I pull into the driveway, I see a strange black Ford truck parked in my spot. I step out and walk up the steps. I open the door and hear a male voice coming from the dining area. The voice seems familiar, but I can't place from where.

As I enter the dining area, I see a muscular guy leaning over the table that is now covered with photos. My mother looks up from the table and spots me standing there, watching.

"Hey, sweetie! This is Linkin. He called because he needs help with clothing designs for his wedding," mom says without making eye contact with me.

She's acting really strange. She keeps looking at this man, and raising her eyebrows.

I walk closer to the table and stop. I lean down and grab one of the photos. When I straighten up, I get a better look at him. He looks to be around six feet tall and built like the Hulk. He has the most gorgeous green eyes and long eyelashes that curl up, making you want to eat him up. His hair is dirty blond and sticks up on top of his head. He has this tight-fitting shirt on with a white priest collar. I have only seen one priest wear it, and that was in the pictures of when I was little and baptized. His skin is so tan, and he is very muscular. He has these thick veins running down both arms. The way he is standing, I can see part of a bumble bee, on his left bicep, peeking out of his sleeve. Another tattoo, down his inner forearm, shows a key with a necklace.

He says something to me, pulling me out of my thoughts.

"I'm sorry. What did you say?" I ask.

"I was asking you if you were up for this big project. My wedding is in a month, and I want my men's outfits to coordinate with the bridesmaids." He flashes a gorgeous smile.

What the hell am I doing. I just survived being abused by a man, and now I am ogling another like he is a piece of chocolate.

I pick up several different pictures of men's vests, sorting them out slowly to give myself time to compose myself. When I take the time to really look at the images in front of me, I let out a giggle. One of the photos I hold up has a black and white snake skin vest with a red rose pinned to it. I place it down and grab another one. This vest is black with white stripes and double rows of white buttons down the center, with a red money sign on the right side of the chest.

"Okay, is this a joke? Because these are the most hideous vests I have ever seen," I can't help but say.

"This is not a joke, Sophia!" he says with a frown, and I instantly regret my comment. "I was told you run a little boutique. I heard great things about you, and that, if anyone could find these unique items my wife and I are looking for, you could."

Okay, now I feel really bad. "I apologize. Sometimes I get verbal diarrhea," I say, placing the picture back on the table.

This will be good for me. It will be my first project since that frightening night. I think getting back out there, and working, will help me move on. I still have nightmares every night. Sometimes I wake up soaking wet with sweat, and my heart is beating really fast. I always wake up when Brad grabs me by the hair to stop me from jumping over the fence to escape. I remember just letting myself fall over the fence onto the pavement. I prayed to God, that night, to let me escape and get down the street for help. I was so scared and started running towards the guys playing basketball two houses down. I didn't realize it, but I was completely naked. One of the guys grabbed his sweatshirt and placed it around me. Another guy covered me with his jacket.

4

Linkin

I CAN'T BELIEVE I am going through with this plan. Sophia looks sexy with her long, brown, wavy hair pulled to one side, over her shoulder. Those brown eyes just sparkle when she laughs, and her smile can light up the whole world. I've never been fascinated with someone's smile, but I just want to put her in a lip-lock. I think faking this wedding is going to be harder to do than we thought, and when she finds out her mother hired me to help her, shit is going to hit the fan. Also, when she finds out I am a chaplain for the military and a counselor, she's really going to be pissed off.

You need to ask God for forgiveness for lying and having sexual thoughts, I remind myself.

"Hello, Linkin, are you here?" Marybeth's voice startles me.

Shoot, I forgot she was going to stop by as my bride to be. I had to use one of my units' wife to play the part of my fiancée because I have been out of the dating game for about two years now. I was close to a relationship with someone but caught her in bed with one of my parishioners.

"Hey, my little love monkey. I was wondering if you would show up," I say, walking towards Marybeth, picking her up, and twirling her around. I sit her back down, grab her hand, and walk her to the table. I hope I am making this believable.

Sophia is frowning at me, but she puts a smile back on and holds her hand out to Marybeth.

"Hi! I am Sophia. I will be designing the groom's suits. Do you want to look at the pictures?" She points towards the pictures displayed on the table.

"Marvelous! I also brought the picture of the wedding dress I want, and I wanted to see if you could find it, or if you have someone in mind to make it." Marybeth hands the picture to Sophia.

I walk to the table and lean over Marybeth's shoulder to get a better look. It is a white wedding dress with a sweetheart shaped top and mermaid bottom made of snake skin. I reach down and pinch the inside of her arm, causing her to yelp.

"Honey, we can get rough in the bedroom later but not now. We need to make sure Sophia is able to help us," she says.

I separate from her and walk around, pretending to look at some other pictures that sit on the far end of the table.

Now, I am no saint, but for the last two years, I've made a deal with God that I will not have any sexual intercourse unless I was one hundred percent sure I found the one.

When I look at Sophia, her mouth is opening and closing. She is trying to find something to say. I am so embarrassed and can't wait for this day to be over with.

"Well!" Sophia finally exclaims. "I am going to make some phone calls and let you know by the end of the week if I can get someone to make this design for you. I don't think there will be any problems doing this."

She makes a couple of calls and writes down several names of people who could find the fabric we need.

One hour later, after some debating back and forth of some of the options she's selected, she's found a promising shop in New York.

"All right, I am going to head out of town to get some of the fabric samples, and I should be back in two days. I really appreciate that you picked me to help with your wedding attire. This will bring more clients to my boutique." She smiles.

"Honey, I have faith you will design the most elegant wedding dress for me," Marybeth says, placing her hand on my bicep.

"Yeah. You're going to do great, and thank you for doing this on such a short notice," I say, motioning to her mother to wrap this up.

"Sophia, we need to get on the road," her mother says, showing us out. "We can stay in a hotel in New York for the night. It's official that you're taking this assignment, so we need to get on top of the orders."

As I walk out the door, I glance back at Sophia. My heart's beating rapidly, seeing her peek around the corner, watching me leave.

Shit, what am I doing? Why can't I say no to this assignment? I want to help her move on, but the bad thing is that my body wants her. I need to go pray for strength and forgiveness.

At work, I go by the secretary's desk to pick up my messages.

"Hey, Chasity, do I have anyone coming in this afternoon?"

"Yes, sir, one gentleman is to arrive at six o'clock. He got into a fight during a drill, breaking one of his partner's arms. The Sargent reports this man beat his partner while on duty," she says.

I nod and go to my office.

Most of the time, I love my job. Sometimes, I hate my job. Once Sophia finds out what I do on top of the lies, it's going to blow up in my face.

I sit back in my chair and open her folder to learn more about her accident. I am hoping that, as we spend more time together, she will start opening up a little. I'll start asking simple questions first.

THE PHONE BUZZES.

"Mr. Garland, Jackson is here to see you, sir," Chasity says.

I push the button.

"Thanks, he can come on in," I say, putting away Sophia's folder.

5

Sophia

I HAVE BEEN in New York for several hours now. Mother and I got a flight out to talk with Zip about the snake skin fabric. Zip owns a boutique here and sells the craziest stuff.

I met him when I came here a year ago, looking for my wedding dress.

✧　✧　✧

HE WAS STANDING in the glass window, dressing one of his mannequin. The dress was cloud blue with a deep V-neck of sheer fabric that flowed down the upper torso, leaving just the light sheer fabric to cover the exposed skin. Light pink flowers covered the sacred parts of the woman's boobs. The dropped waistline was ruffled up with cloud blue fabric, silver sequins, and layers of the light pink flowers. In the center, just below the belly button, there was a three-inch light pink bow with a silver heart in the middle. The dress was floor-length, and the light pink flowers looked like they were climbing up the sequins halfway up the dress. I stood there, just amazed at how beautiful this dress was.

Zip, who had black, skinny smart crop pants and black loafers on with a silver buckle on the top, had turned around. His shirt was a mustard yellow slim fit. He was tall and slim, and his skin was a russet color. He looked at us and waved for us to come in. Brad grabbed my arm and dragged me into the store.

He was so excited to finally move forward with the wedding. I had told him I wanted to make sure we could live together first. When we entered, the place was filled with so many colorful dresses; I just stopped and gazed in wonderment.

"How can I help you, darling?" the gentleman said with a huge smile that showed off his perfect, white teeth.

"My fiancé and I are looking for someone to help us find a dress. I am searching for a one-shoulder ball gown with a chapel train and black taffeta and tulle. Then his tux was going to be black with a cream vest with black buttons."

The shop keeper looked at me with glowing eyes, and I knew right away we were on the same page with our tastes.

✧   ✧   ✧

"Sophia! Oh my god, girl, where have you been?" Zip says, giving me a big hug and a kiss on the cheek.

He couldn't stand Brad. He always told me he got a bad vibe from him.

"Been in the hospital," I say as tears form in my eyes.

My mother exchanges a look with Zip, but I can't help it; I loved Brad so much, and I still can't believe he was capable of doing that.

"Come here," Zip says, hugging me again and rubbing my back.

I tell him what happened while mother goes to look at some fabrics.

"If I knew how to fight, I would have cut his dick off and let him watch me suck it," he says once he's heard all the horrific details.

I giggle. This man is hilarious.

"Thank you, Zip, but he wasn't worth it. It's going to take some time. He hurt me really bad, and the worse thing is, I still love him," I say.

"Well, baby girl, time heals, and you will be able to move on one day. When you do move on, you're going to look back and think, 'I almost married that jackass,'" he says, leading me back to his Goddess room by the hand. That's what he calls his dress room.

I start pulling several different dresses and some left-over fabric from a rack, glad for the diversion. After I send several pictures to Linkin and Marybeth, they choose what they want.

We hug and thank Zip before heading out to call a taxi. Our flight is not for another hour. We decide to grab a hot dog from the man outside the building while waiting for the ride.

While I spin around, taking in this busy street of New York, this woman flies past me, screaming that a man is trying to kill her. A wave of dread washes over me as I turn my head in the direction she's pointing, and there is this man on a bicycle, waving a gun, heading straight towards me.

I stand there, in shock, unable to move, and my mother pushes me out of the way. I start feeling a tingle in my legs and find myself sweating profusely. I can't catch my breath.

Out of nowhere, someone grabs my arm. I turn around fast and find myself staring into Brad's eyes. I step back, turn around, and run down the street as fast as I can. I hear people hollering and vehicles beeping their horns. I see the curb in front of me, so I jump down and feel a sharp pain between my legs.

When I glance down, I see a lot of blood dripping

down my legs onto the street. All of a sudden, I hear a roaring in my ears, and my heart is beating very fast. I get weak in the knees and feel myself dropping down to the ground. I am hearing sirens blaring and someone hollering my name, but I can't focus. My body hits the pavement, and I close my eyes, hoping that someone will come help me.

I'VE BEEN IN the hospital for three days. I was told my uterus prolapsed, and the ligaments that support the uterus have been torn again, and that surgery won't be able to correct it. The surgeon ended up doing a hysterectomy but left my ovaries. The area where they sewed my vagina to my anus two months ago opened back up. I will have to wear a wound VAC for several weeks to help it stay sterile and heal properly.

My mother told me that I had a panic attack after the scene of the man chasing the woman with a gun. This caused me to have a flashback, and I thought it was Brad.

There is a knock on the door. I look around the half-open curtain around my bed, and see Linkin standing in the corridor with a bouquet of rainbow roses and lilies. He is dressed in camouflage hunting pants and a solid white shirt.

"Have you been hunting?" I ask to break the awkward silence.

"No, these are my work clothes. I was doing my training exercises when I got the call about you. I booked a flight out right away and headed to see you."

"Well, my mother told me Marybeth still wants to use me for your wedding attire. I had surgery and will be on bed rest for six weeks, but I can still work from my bed. It will keep me from getting bored. I found the fabric to make your vest and Marybeth's wedding dress," I say, pointing toward the bag sitting on top of the window sill.

He walks over, grabs the bag, and walks over to the chair beside my bed and sits down.

He places the bag on his lap and pulls out the snake skin fabric.

"This means a lot to Marybeth and me that you still want to help us." He looks at me for a moment before adding. "If you're not up for it, I can find someone else."

I quickly sit up, forgetting about just having surgery. I let out a wrenching scream, falling back down on the bed. Linkin is already out of his chair, trying to help me get situated. His large muscular hand grabs my inner arm and lifts me up gently in the bed. The cotton hospital gown has slipped up above my mid-thigh. I push it down quickly so he doesn't see all my scars.

"Are you okay?" he asks, looking at me with concern.

"That hurt like hell. I am going to buzz the nurse for some pain medication," I say, touching the call button.

He sits down on the edge of the bed and grabs my hand. I feel an electrical spark when we touch. I thought this would scare me, but I like his touch.

"Sophia, I have something to tell you, and I want you to know that I don't want to lie to you anymore," he says.

I try to pull my hand away, but he keeps a tight hold on it. I feel a sense of dread settling in as he tells me what he and my mother had planned.

"I wanted to let you know that your mother called me after your abuse from your boyfriend. She asked me to come help you. She didn't think you would want my help when you refused the help of several psychiatrists, counselors, and priests. I made up the wedding to get closer to you and help you move on," he says.

I pull my hand from his and close my eyes, counting to eight while breathing in and out. How dare my mother meddle in my life? I can't believe she thought a military priest could help me. I was beaten, raped, and stabbed. A guy I loved, who was in the military, just flips, one night, and tries to kill me. Why does this man think he can ever get me to trust him? I am so pissed right now I am shaking.

"GET OUT! I want you to get out and never contact me again," I say.

"Please, listen to me," he says, "I want to help you, Sophia. I watched a woman in my camp get brutally beaten and raped by multiple men. I was told if I tried to tell anyone that they would kill me. I went to the military hospital where Rae was being taken care of, to talk to her. I would visit her every day, but she refused my help. One day I was prepared to argue with her, but the innocent woman had died. I felt it was my fault because I should've pushed harder to share my word with her. I made a promise to God that day. If I got a second chance to help someone, I would do anything in my power to succeed in helping that person."

Our eyes meet, and I grab his hand. His eyes tell me how sincere he is, but I have to push him away.

"Goodbye, Linkin. I don't need or want your help. I forgive you for lying to me. I know you were doing what you thought was best to help me, but I need you to leave and not bother me again," I whisper sadly.

He frowns and shakes his head. He leaned over, closer to me, and kisses my forehead. He reaches into his pocket, pulls out a can of pepper spray and a bible. He places the items on the table beside my bed.

"I brought this for you today. I want you to take these and carry them wherever you go. The bible is to open when you need guidance, and the pepper spray is for protection." He looks at me one last time before turning around and walking to the door. When he opens it, he mouths *sorry* and walks out, shutting it behind him.

6

Linkin

I SHOULD'VE KNOWN better than to think she would be okay with the honesty. The moment I told her it was a lie, her lip started to tremble. The way she pushed my hand away from her and yelled for me to get out makes me flinch. I was exhausted from all the drills we'd done at work and then from being on a plane for several hours. I am going to give her some time and then become a pest in her life.

I walk into the café down the street. I need to get some caffeine and some food before getting back on a plane. I call Marybeth to tell her the fake wedding is off, and she is not very happy. Dean takes the phone from her to ask me what happened.

"Damn, man, you should have just kept the secret until she started to open up, and she might have been okay with the lie," he says.

"Dean, she had to have her uterus taken out," I explain. "This woman is only in her thirties, and she can't have children. I don't think waiting to tell the truth would have made a difference."

I cover the mouthpiece to give the barista my order and go sit down in a window seat.

I look out the window, watching how crowded the streets are here, and thinking about what Sophia went through hearing all the different noises this city makes. Any person who went through a traumatic experience can have PTSD and should not be around a lot of noise.

"Hello, earth to Linkin," Dean says.

His voice pulls me out of my trance.

"Sorry, man, I was thinking about stuff."

The barista is calling my name for my order.

"Hey, Dean, I've got to go. I'll call you later."

"FLIGHT SEVEN-SEVEN-SEVEN IS now boarding at gate ten," I hear over the intercom.

I get out of my seat and head to the gate.

The plane ride home is quiet. I decide to take a nap and think of my plan to get Sophia to talk to me again.

I PULL UP at my house and unlock my door. I hear Max's paws stomping to the door. Max is a white boxer with one brown ring around his left eye. I found him in the woods on my morning jog two years ago. He was lying on the ground, whining. When I walked over to him, I noticed he had a large gash on his back leg. I took him home to clean the leg and sew it up. When you're in the military, you are taught how to survive in the woods, and sewing yourself up was part of the teachings.

I go down the hall, heading to take a shower. I hate being on the plane with all these people coughing up a lung and spreading their germs. I reach over and turn on the water, letting it get warm while I undress. I feel something in my back pocket and reach back there to see what it is. It's my credit card and receipt from where I got Sophia's flowers. I place them on the sink and walk in my shower.

I grab the shampoo, squirt some in my hand, and start lathering it in my hair. I close my eyes and let my mind wander off. I think back to when I told Sophia the truth and when she reached out and touched my hand. I know we both felt the connection. I lean back and let the water run down my hair, and the soap suds slide down my body. I let my right hand glide down my stomach; my dick is hard. I wrap my hand around the base and start working it up and down. With my eyes closed, I imagine it's Sophia's hand. She lowers her mouth and slowly puts the tip in and swirls her tongue around it. She takes my dick all the way in and sucks hard coming back up.

The pressure in my balls is building up, and my dick is pulsating as I imagine her hand moving faster around my dick while her mouth works the top. She takes her other hand and cups my balls as I reach the edge of pleasure.

I open my eyes and realize that I just beat my meat thinking of Sophia. I feel ashamed. I acted out my male instinct instead of remaining faithful to God.

I wash myself off then rinse down the shower before cutting the water off. I step out of the shower and head to the bedroom to put my boxers on.

As I'm lying down on my bed, looking up at the ceiling, my brain won't stop thinking about her, and I know I must find a way to see her again.

THE NEXT FEW days are very busy. I am dealing with several soldiers who watched one of their own beat his wife at the barracks. There were several complaints that the soldiers heard a woman scream. One of the soldiers went outside and saw Craig punching is wife in the face. He said her body looked like a rag doll being beat on the ground. He says he grabbed him and pulled him off. The commander called me, saying counseling is needing as soon as possible. The wife has brought the military in on the actions of her husband.

Since this was domestic violence, he will be punished. The military declared a "zero tolerance" policy. I am to counsel him and take the appropriate steps to prevent domestic violence happening again. I feel like the person should take responsibility for his actions and work on controlling his anger.

I am sitting at my desk, going over Craig's file when there is a knock at the door. My secretary, Chasity, cracks open the door and sticks her head in.

"Craig is here for his appointment," she says.

I wave, signaling I am ready to see him, and she opens the door to escort him in. This guy is wearing basketball shorts, a Game Cock shirt, and a black sun visor. He looks to be around six feet and has very broad shoulders. I remember his wife looked to be about five feet tall and very curvy. Just to think of this large man hitting that small-framed wife of his makes me want to come around the desk and whoop his ass. I don't agree with a man laying a hand on a woman. I think there are too many coping mechanisms to reach for before you just swing a fist. But this is my job, and I am not here to judge him.

I place his chart down on the desk and walk around to greet him. I stand there for a second, giving him time to get comfortable on the recliner. I use my dad's old chair as my patient's seat because it is so cushy, and people seem to enjoy it. I sit down across from him and lean both elbows on my upper thighs. I notice this kind of helps patients be more comfortable with me.

"Hey, Craig, my name is Reverend Garland. I am glad to meet you," I say, starting the conversation. "How are you doing today?" On the first day, I try to make small talk and not overwhelm the patient.

"Nice to meet you, sir. I am doing all right. My wife has moved out for a while, until you give me a clearance that I am okay." He sounds sad.

"So, tell me, what caused you to become so angry that day?"

"I've been going to see the on-base doctor for my migraines. They put me on some Imitrex to see if that will help. At first, it was working, but then I noticed that, after taking the shot, I would get this funny sensation down my face and neck. The doctor told me that it's a normal side effect, and it should go away after a few minutes.

"The morning of the accident, I had a bad migraine. I was very sensitive to light and noises, and my children were hollering and arguing about school. I grabbed my oldest son and pushed him on the couch and told him to shut up. Nina, my wife, came barging into the living room, cussing at me. We had some heated arguments, and I left.

"When I got to work, I took the Imitrex. We did a

couple of drills, but I wasn't feeling any better, and I told them I would be right back. When I entered my barracks, I went to get some water and take the second Imitrex. I was told to take it after two hours if the first one didn't take away the migraine."

"Sorry to interrupt, but why would you have a bunk in the barracks if you are staying at home?" I ask, curious.

"The commander told me to just use one of those beds if a migraine came on. I stay at home but just use an empty bed on base," he explains.

"Okay, that is understandable. You can continue telling me about that day."

"So, I went to take the second Imitrex and lay across the bed. My phone was ringing in my pants. I reached down and took it out of my pocket, and it was the guard, saying Nina was here. I told him it was okay for her to come in. She came in and sat on the bed opposite of mine. She was fussing about my temper and about the chronic migraines I am having. We were arguing and then things just went black. I don't remember anything after that, until one of the other soldiers was pulling me off my wife." His whole body's shaking.

"Okay, that's enough for today. You did well. How do you feel?" I ask.

"It felt good to get that off my chest," Craig says.

"I want to let you know that anger can be destructive. We first need to recognize what sets you off. You need to find several practical methods that you can practice daily to reduce your anger and prevent it from rising. I am going to contact the doctor over there, and get some more information on Imitrex. In the meantime, I wrote out some anger management skill cards for you to take home with you to practice." I hand him four cards.

He shuffles through them, looking at each one.

He takes a deep breath and stands up. I stand up, matching him, and hold my hand out. We shake hands, I hand him his next appointment date, and he waves as he exits through the door.

I walk back over to my desk to finish my notes on Craig, but I start thinking about Sophia and the ex-boyfriend who stabbed her, raped her, and beat her until he thought she was dead. I have gone through his background files, police charges, and even contacted all his other girlfriends. I wanted to see if he's shown any anger toward them. He has a very clean record. Everyone I have spoken to says how good of a man he was and how what happened was a big shock to them all.

I do know that he is in jail for a long time, but he's trying to use his PTSD to get away with what happened. It hadn't occurred to me that he could succeed. I am going to make some phone calls and make sure he never gets out.

7

Linkin

Six months later

"SO, CRAIG, ARE you ready to finish our last session today?" I ask.

"Reverend Garland, I have one question to ask you before we start," he says.

"Sure, Craig, what is it?"

"I want to know if I can continue my care after this session is done. My wife has agreed to come back home if I continue."

"That's understandable. After the inquiry into what happened, the doctor found out that Imitrex's side effects can trigger anger outbursts and might have affected your mood. I have cleared you for the PTSD. When you talk to your wife, ask her if she would like to join you during the sessions. Sometimes it helps couples, and it gives her some insight on how you cope with anger," I suggest.

"That would be great! So, let's get this session done, sir."

CRAIG AND I are walking out together to the parking lot when my phone vibrates. I wave bye to Craig, heading toward my car.

"Reverend Garland here," I answer.

"Hey, Reverend Garland, this is Commanding Officer Hooks calling to tell you you're being deployed to Fairbanks, Alaska," a strong voice informs me.

I am stunned.

"Yes, sir, I will pack my stuff and head over for the paperwork."

I haven't been deployed for a while now. I have a bad feeling about this, but this is my job, and I took an oath.

ON THE WAY home, I stop by the store to get several of my favorite snacks to take with me. I get the urge to call Sophia while in the car, and right away, I get her voicemail. I leave her a message, telling her I am just checking up on her and making sure she is okay. I tell her I am being deployed to Alaska to fight the uprising of the Grizzly bears. Then I go on and tell her it's a joke, but I *am* being deployed, and I would like to skype with her sometime if she is okay with that.

I'M SITTING ON the plane, looking out the window. The man beside me is huge, and half his stomach is on my side of the seat. His elbow keeps hitting my arm. I am debating if I should say something, but I close my eyes and take a couple of deep breaths. The stewardess comes by, asking if we need anything, and I shake my head yes. I need to get out of this seat.

"Judy, I see there is an empty seat up front. I need to make several prayers for the Navy before I reach them. I was wondering if I could move up." I flash her my best smile.

"Yes, sir, we have one seat in first class if you would like that," she says.

Heck, who's going to argue with that.

The flight attendant escorts me to my new seat. I lay down my hand bag, my book, and computer on the table next to me. I sit down in this huge seat, and it fully reclines back. As I am settling in my chair, another flight attendant comes up with a menu for me to order a five-course meal.

"Sir, would you like champagne, water, tea, or orange juice?"

"Sure, I'll take a sweet tea." I answer. This is so much fun.

For my main course I choose steak, mashed potatoes, and asparagus. I go with the house salad and New York Cheese Cake with fresh strawberries.

For the next four hours of my flight, I lie back in the recliner and take a nap. I am startled when the pilot comes on the intercom to announce some turbulence from the heavy snow fall and wind. I settle back up in a sitting position and pull out my phone. I see a missed call from Sophia. I get up to walk to the restroom and dial her number.

After the third ring, she picks up. "Hello," she says.

"Hey! I just saw you called. I'm on the plane and wanted to talk."

"Crap! You know you can't talk on the phone when you're on a plane. It messes with the electronics," she whispers.

"Well, I am in the bathroom right now. I just wanted to clean the air between us, and I really want us to be friends. I was hoping, when I get back home, we could hang out a little. I am not going to counsel you, but if you ever need to talk, I am here." I hope I didn't say too much.

She laughs a little. "Okay, I'll let you finish your bathroom break. Oh, and I would like to be your friend. I'll send you my skype address."

I wash my hands and head back to my chair. I place all my items back in my bag and sit down. I close my eyes for the rest of the ride with a smile on my face.

Why should I care to be friends with Sophia? It's not like we could be a couple one day. My chest gets heavy with anger when I think back to her chart. How can someone hurt this special girl? In all my years of working as a Chaplain, this is the worst case I've seen. After a lot of digging and coming up with nothing, I have decided to go visit her attacker soon. He won't know who I am. The guards in jail know what I do for a living. They'll think I'm coming just to counsel the prisoner, but I need to look into his eyes and hear his version of what happened.

AN HOUR LATER, I arrive at Fort Benson. At the main entrance, there are three security guards lined up in full cold-weather gear, holding guns. I hear that this is the coldest area in Alaska.

"U.S. army Chaplain Garland here, called for duty," I say, handing over my badge to one of the guards.

His lips press tight as he takes it from my hand. "All right, sir. Malcom here will take you to the housing service office where you'll fill out your paperwork."

I step forward, and soldier Malcom nods his head and turns to head straight through the gate. I notice that this base is between two snow-capped mountains.

"Chaplain Garland, sir," Malcom says as he opens the door to this brick building.

He walks me toward a horseshoe-shaped table with a five-person crew that sit behind their computers.

"Army Lt. Col. Brent McDaniel. This is Chaplain Garland. He was assigned to our base, sir," Malcom explains as he waits to be cleared to stand down.

"Thank you, Malcom. I'll take it from here."

"Thank you, sir." Malcom turns and marches outside.

After half an hour of paperwork, I follow the Lt. to the chapel. He stops at building eight-forty-five.

"This is where you will stay." He hands me a packet. "There is a map inside. The blue paper tells you the soldiers' schedule. We like for everyone to eat together, and this yellow paper tells you the location, menu, and the times." The Lt. turns to unlock the door.

I walk in to smell a wet, musky smell. The walls are covered in natural antique wood paneling. The wood's a mixture of different types of trees. I follow the wall up to the vaulted ceiling that is also made of wood but of a lighter color. I move down the center aisle and see light wooden benches on both sides. The carpet looks like it used to be a cream color, but the brown smudges of many feet trampling over it for years have permanently changed its hue.

I walk farther down the aisle and sweep my eyes to a painted stained glass window in the corner of the chapel. The glass is made up with a three-dimensional structure. The colors make the room stand out. The vertical windows are stained with purple, blue, red, and white. These were clearly made by some artist because the pictures are beautifully illuminated with Bible stories.

"Chaplin Garland, we appreciate you coming here to help our guys. It's been a year since someone has preached here," Lt. McDaniel says, breaking my contemplation.

"Sir, I love my job," I say. "I will do my best to help. When we head to dinner, I'll do my duty by standing to offer my services to them all." I square my shoulders and lift my head. I was taught to stand tall when in the presence of authority.

"Excellent, Rev. Garland, see you at nineteen hundred. The chef is preparing a nice meal to welcome you to base," Lt. says as he turns and heads out the front door.

I am exhausted from the plane ride. There is a light on toward the front of the church. I pick up my bag and head that way. Once I get to the stage, I can see a wooden door on the right. As soon as I open the door, the cold brutal air slaps my face. Someone must have opened a window to help with the mildew smell. The heat is running loudly to compensate for all this cold air running inside. I walk over to the window to shut it, but I stop when I see a woman doing clap pushups on the snow-covered ground. She looks to be around thirty. She jumps up, both hands reaching for the sky, then she jumps down for the pushup, coming half-way up and clapping. I am really mesmerized by how good she is.

"Do you like what you see, Chaplain, sir?" she says, out of breath.

I shake my head and lower the window down. I know I'll have to explain myself soon, but I need some rest. I grab my sleeping bag out of the luggage pile, and lay it down on the bed. As I reach to take my boots off, I notice Sophia's business card. I lie down on the bed, with my boots hanging off, and hold the card up to just look at her beautiful, angelic face.

I JERK AWAKE from a loud, piercing ringing of a bell. When I look over at my cell, it says seven o'clock. I needed that one-hour nap from jet lag, but now I am late for dinner.

After taking a five-minute shower and freezing when I get out without a towel, I grab my pajama bottoms to dry myself off, then I get ready. I take one more glance at myself, to make sure I am dressed correctly. I place my white clerical collar necktie on and head out to dinner.

As I step into the dining hall, I see the same woman who was working out behind the chapel, standing at the door with her hands behind her back.

"So glad you could make it, Chaplain Garland," she says with a sarcastic smile.

"Sorry for being late. I fell asleep. The twelve-hour flight here wore me out," I say as I hold out my hand to shake hers.

I am somewhat surprised when she holds out her hand.

"Just giving you a hard time, sir," she responds with a big smile. "I was given specific orders to show you around. I am Sergeant Darcy Armstrong."

I follow her to a table with several soldiers. All the tables are full of women and men. After introducing myself to a few people, I head to the front and turn so I am facing all the soldiers.

"Hello, everyone. I am Chaplain Linkin Garland. I was assign to this post. I am here to guide you in your worship but also to listen. I want to thank each and every one of you for serving our country. I will lead our meal in prayer, and then we can dig in," I say, and all hands in the room start to clap.

It feels good to be back. I went to school and

learned the word of prayer to help others.

"Dear Heavenly Father, we bow our heads to give you thanks for giving us this food for nourishment. Thank you for meeting our physical needs of hunger and thirst. Forgive us for taking that simple joy for granted, and bless this meal to fuel our bodies. We pray that this food will energized us to be able to work for the glory of your Kingdom. In Jesus' name we pray. Amen." I open my eyes and give the thumbs up to eat.

8

Linkin

THE FOLLOWING DAY, I head for breakfast. I enter and head to the spot from last night to do the prayer before the meal. After the prayer, I sit down beside Darcy and Malcom. I lean forward to grab a piece of toast from the basket, and as I reach for the jelly, my arm brushes against Darcy's.

"I apologize. I just needed some jelly," I say sincerely and lean back to my original position, worried I'm making things worse.

"Chaplain Garland, sir. It's okay. We all get over-excited about jelly," she says with a laugh.

When all the soldiers at my table laugh with her, I join in.

As the soldiers discuss their duties for the day, I sit there and listen openly. They discuss how they will break up into four teams and practice drills against each other in case of an attack. I found out this eight-hundred-acre base is one of the only two missile-defense complexes in the country.

Darcy goes on to discuss the training mission for her team. Her team is heading down to the underground silo house that holds the missiles. She explains how they are used for testing and as back up in case of an emergency.

"ALL RIGHT, GUYS and girls. We are heading outside for our morning exercise. I have brought everyone an insulated face mask. The temperature outside is twenty degrees, but the wind chill is what will get you," Darcy mentions while she hands out the masks.

Once she gets in front of me, she leans down to my face. "Chaplain Garland, do you have what it takes to follow?" Her voice is strong and confident.

I place both hands on the table and push myself up. We are both face to face, but I am still in her personal space. She thinks, since she is in charge of her team, her authority extends over me as well.

"Sergeant Armstrong, you might be the team leader for your men, but I am a team leader for God." I say this just to get back at her for the jelly joke. "But, I believe I will follow your group today, to learn the ropes around here. If our country gets attacked, I want to know what I can do to help and to protect myself."

She steps back and puts her hands behind her back, but she grounds herself, and I can tell her adrenaline is pumping just by watching her carotid artery beating on the side of her neck. I watch as she swallows her anger and gives me a genuine smile. Oh, boy, I am in trouble now.

AN HOUR LATER, we are out in the Alaska woods behind the base. Darcy takes us up a mountain trail. All soldiers are carrying a weapon except for me. I do have my sterling silver cross around my neck. I hope God is watching out for all of us.

The snow is coming down heavily. The walkie-talkie Darcy has on her hip forecasts the weather. The man speaks loudly, alerting the town that a snowstorm is coming. The trees are coated with snow, and cast shadows throughout the trail. The wind is whistling, and all we can hear is the snow crunching under our salty winter boots.

I watch the soldiers follow behind Darcy in a jog, and imagine the sound of men and women panting from the three miles up a mountain.

I feel a satisfaction and physical high during the run. While jogging, I brainstorm on how to find more information about Brad. I need to figure out who to talk with that could pull some history on him. I have to make sure I don't do anything illegal or jeopardize someone's job. For some reason, I think back to my past with Carly. I haven't seen her in a long time, and even though we both decided to part ways because of our career choices, she was the first woman who questioned my job. I know that a Chaplain can be married, but your partner needs to be one hundred percent dedicated to God as well. Carly was beautiful, with her long blond hair, and her ocean blue eyes had the longest eyelashes I have ever seen. They made her blue eyes pop. It was at my niece's school, where I was asked to speak for career day, that I fell in love with the teacher, only to be crushed when she decided that being in a military relationship was too hard. She wanted a man who was home every night.

I feel a sharp pain in my calf. I snap out of my daydream to realize I'm at least a mile from the group. I see Darcy heading my way. I bend down to rub my right calf. Darn. My leg feels like it's on fire. I must have pulled a muscle going up the steep hill.

"What the hell, sir! Did you not hear me hollering?" Darcy says, letting go of my arm she had grabbed.

"Sorry. I think a lot when I run and block out everything else," I mumble under my breath.

"Let me get a look at your calf," she says as she squats down to examine my leg.

She lifts up my pants leg and long john. Her hand

is moving softly around the calf.

"Your skin is hot to the touch and swollen. I think the doctor will need to look at it. It could be a pulled muscle, since you didn't stretch, or it could be a blood clot."

Not sure how to respond, I just nod then pull down my pants leg. She stands back up, and I follow back down the hill with a limp, somewhat ashamed that they all have to cut their exercise short because of me.

After an hour of walking, we arrived back to the base. Darcy has called the doctor and told him to meet us at the gate. I am put on an old stretcher bed and carried to the military treatment facility. An ultrasound is done on my calf and shows no blood clot or damage, thankfully. I am given direction to ice it for twenty minutes every hour and keep it elevated. I think my pride was hurt more than my leg.

I AM AWOKEN by my phone's ringing beside my bed. I pick it up and can't help the smile that appears on my lips. Sophia's beautiful face shows on facetime, but then I notice she's frowning. We haven't spoken in a few days.

"Hey! Sophia are you okay?" I ask, concerned. I know something must have happened for her to call me first.

"I had another nightmare. I was hoping we could talk. The psychiatrist I see creeps me out," she admits and her lip trembles.

It makes me want to fly back and just hold her in my arms.

Oh, God, I don't need these thoughts.

I can see the fear and terror roll off her body. She is trembling, and her hands keep moving up and down her arms.

I put on my professional face. "Okay, let's start from the beginning. What did you do the day of the nightmare?" I ask.

9

Sophia

I CAN'T BELIEVE I'm dialing Linkin on facetime, but I've decided the psychiatrist is not helping my PTSD. After months of therapy and my nightmares only getting worse, I've decided maybe Linkin can help. So, I plan to facetime him because, for some strange reason, I want to see him.

I close my eyes, take a deep breath, and hit the call button. I clear my throat and sigh, trying to calm my nerves. For a long moment, I stare at his whiskered face. His hair has grown around his jaw and above his lip. He looks different but happy.

I give him a weak smile.

"Hi!" My heart is beating very fast, and I have chills down both arms. I rub both arms up and down to create friction to warm up.

I bet he thinks I'm a nut case. I pushed him away

even after he told me the truth. I was angry and frustrated that I was lied to, but also, I liked him and that scared me.

"Hey, Sophia, are you okay?" he asks with concern in his voice.

Damn my nerves. I stopped my anxiety medication, and I have not slept in days. After dosing off for about an hour, I woke up in sweats from a nightmare where Brad had broken in my house and tried to kill me again.

"I've been having problems sleeping for weeks now. The psychiatrist wrote a prescription to help me rest during the night," I admit in a weak voice. "This dream was the worst of them all. Brad killed me."

"Would you like to tell me about the dream? I think your body finally relaxed after suffering from lack of sleep, but one of the side effects of that is unusual dreams."

"The dream felt so real. I was on the couch, wrapped in a blanket, watching a lifetime movie. I guess I must have dosed off, because Brad was suddenly across the room, reclined back in the chair with the gun pointed at me," I say as I wipe a tear that falls on my cheek.

Linkin is sitting there, with a pillow behind his head. It appears the walls are some kind of wood. His gaze is so intense, waiting for me to finish talking.

I nod and continue my story. "He said, 'You're my Angel. Why couldn't you love me?'" I start to tremble at the memory, but I force myself to continue. "Brad got up from the chair and walked over to the couch. He stood there with the gun still aimed at me. When I tried to talk, he placed the gun in my mouth. He clicked off the safety and whispered, 'MINE.'" As I finish my story, I drop the phone and stumble to the bathroom to vomit. I flush the toilet, turn on the water, and rinse my mouth out.

When I'm sure I'm not going to throw up again, I reach for the phone in my room and see Linkin's face close up to the camera. I can see he is standing now and must be outside because I see the snow in the light from the post behind him.

"You're okay. Calm down. Take a breath in. That's it, hold it … count one, two, three, four, five, six, seven, and eight. Okay, now, breathe out. That's it, you're doing good," he says in a soothing voice.

I needed that. I lean back on the headboard and close my eyes. I feel relieved and safe. This man, the Chaplain who is across the world in Alaska, just helped me from having a panic attack. I think talking to him might possibly help.

"Linkin, thank you so much for listening. I shouldn't have been so cruel when you tried to apologize. I am sorry for that, and I am asking you for help," I grip the phone tightly, waiting for his response.

"Absolutely, I'll help. Let's talk once a week. That will give you some time to start writing in a journal." He makes his way back inside from the cold.

I hear him shuffling some kind of papers on a wooden desk.

"So, I know you don't think this will benefit you, but it helps with coping skills. Physically, journaling can reduce the tension in your body and help you focus on the triggers." He holds up his hand to stop me from protesting just yet. "First thing I want you to do is go out and find a journal that attracts you. It's always easier if you have some kind of decorated book that you enjoy looking at. Next, I want you to choose a quiet place to sit, where no noise, people, or animals are around to distract you. Then, I want you to start with this first question I am about to ask you. I don't want you to talk to me about it. I want you to write it down." His voice is stern.

I can tell he is in his work mode now.

"Number one. Did I consciously and willfully do something bad or unfair to deserve to be hurt? This is your first assignment question," he states.

I have tears streaming down my face. I place my hand over my mouth to quieten the sob. How dare he start with such an emotional question? But I asked for his help, so I am going to pull up my big-girl panties and try.

"Yes, I'll work on the first question, but I want you to know I don't like this question at all," I say with a hiccup.

"This is a very hard question, but I like to start with this one because everyone goes over this in their head when something wrong happens in their life."

"Hello? Chaplain Garland, are you in here?" a female voice hollers out.

I see him turn his head with a surprised look on his face. My body goes rigid. I want to know who this woman is. Why is this woman in his place without having knocked first?

In the distance, I see a very petite blond whose hair is hanging down in curls. She has on a brown turtle neck with a camouflage vest. She's beautiful. She looks to be around thirty.

"I need to talk to you, sir," she calls out, standing there, with her hands behind her back.

"Hey, Sophia, I need to go, but mark down one week from now to call for your next session," Linkin says, glancing back in the direction where the blond is standing and then back to me. "Remember, if you need to talk then call me."

I can't help but smile. In the little time I have known him, I've come to believe he truly would stop everything to help me.

"Yes, sir, I will put a reminder in my phone. I'll give the journal writing a try. I'll talk to you later. Bye!" I say in a rush and hit the end button before he can say more.

I take a deep breath and slowly blow it out. I drop my head back on the headboard of my bed. When I look out the window and notice that the sun has gone down, I decide to head downstairs to see what mom is cooking and also to tell her I finally got the nerve to call Linkin.

I head to the kitchen, following the smell of chicken casserole. This is one of my favorite meals since I was a child. I bet, if I look in the pot on the stove, I'll find out she's also cooked me green peas. She's been cooking all my favorites lately because I have lost twenty pounds from the stress of the nightmares and lack of sleep. I've been so depressed from my hysterectomy as well. My heart hurts just thinking about how I won't be able to have kids of my own.

I walk over to mom leaning over the sink, washing off some strawberries. I wrap my arms around her middle and place my chin on her shoulder.

"I love you no matter what, and I am sorry for being such a bitch to you," I say, squeezing her tighter.

She places her hands on mine and lightly taps

them. "You are my whole world, baby girl, and I would do anything in my power to help you. My heart just aches for you, and I thought getting Linkin to help was in your best favor. I didn't mean to upset you. Please forgive me?" She sobs and her body shakes.

"Mom, I forgive you, and I took a step tonight and facetimed him. I have asked him to counsel me, and he said yes."

She turns around so quickly I stumble back, but I steady myself before falling.

"Oh my gosh…that is great," she says with a huge smile.

"One step at a time, mom. After dinner we need to go shopping for the perfect journal."

10

Linkin

I WANTED MORE…I wanted to reach through the phone and touch her, to make her feel protected. But I couldn't do that, and I don't understand why I have feelings for her other than as her chaplain. Dear God. I am in so much trouble.

"Chaplain Garland, are you okay?" Darcy asks.

I forgot that she was here.

I turn around to address her, and she is too close, in my personal space. I back up, forgetting the bed is behind me, and my heels hit the bottom of the bed, causing my back to hit the mattress.

"Holy shit!" she says with a giggle before sitting down on the bed, beside me.

I stiffen. "Was there something you needed, Sergeant Armstrong?" I ask, and when I look at her, I see a flash of interest.

"We were expecting you for dinner to bless the food, but you never showed up. I just stopped by to make sure you were okay," she says as she looks around my small bedroom. "I also wanted to check your leg out." She slides off the bed and pulls up my pants leg. Her hands move up the back of my calf, and her fingers press in and out in circles.

"That's enough," I say, standing, and walk to the other side of the room.

She rises up and heads toward me. I hold out my hand to signal her to stop.

"I am so sorry, sir. I was just trying to help. I crossed the line, and again, I am so sorry," she says before turning and running out of my room.

I sit back down on the bed and place both elbows on my upper thighs and rest my head in my hands. I need to talk with her. She needs to know I am a man of God, and my job is to focus on their well-being and guide them when they need help. But I can see she wants more than I can give.

I stand up and quietly make my way to the chapel. I walk across the wooden stage to the pew. I sit down and look over to the massive pipes that line the wall to the left, where the organ sits. I can tell from the dust that has formed on top of it that it's been a long time since someone has played it. To the right sits an old wooden acoustic piano and above is a magnificent colorful stained glass that sparkles from the light of the lamppost outside.

I think back to my first day on the job and of the chaplain who I followed during my internship in my last year of college.

✦　✦　✦

HE SAID, "SON, your first assignment is to provide ministry and care to a wounded soldier. The soldier lost his leg to a roadside bomb."

I will never forget the rage in the guy's eyes. I could feel the anger that rolled off his body like the waves of an ocean, crashing on the sand. My anxiety spiked as I walked over to him. I stood there and pulled myself together and prayed to God that what comes out of my mouth will be the right thing.

"Lt. Luke Smith, I am Chaplain Linkin Garland. I am here to provide care and counseling," I said, standing at attention.

"I don't want you here," he replied, and I still stood at attention.

I knew what he was doing. He felt guilt, anger, and his impulses told him to hide his feelings.

"Look, I know what kind of obstacles you are about to endure. I am a man of God, and I am here to help you emotionally, physically, mentally, and spiritually. I am going to be here till the end of rehabilitation. So you are stuck with me." I embraced him with a smile.

He looked up at me and grunted. "I can try. But I'm warning you that I am pissed off at the world right now. This was my first year on tour, and I didn't even get to serve my country."

"Lt. Smith, you did serve your country. You want to know how?" I asked, waiting to see if he will reply.

"How! I was bombed on the side of the road. I didn't get to shoot a terrorist. So, please, explain how I served my country?" he hollered out in frustration.

The army nurse pulled back the curtain with concern.

I waved her off, and she pulled the curtain closed again. "Just because you didn't bring violence on the enemy, it doesn't mean you weren't there to protect us. You chose to fight for our country, to protect us from the enemy, and in God's book, you won." I noticed his eyes become clouded with wet tears, but he quickly blinked to hide them.

✧ ✧ ✧

I HEAR VOICES outside, and that brings me back to reality. I look down at my watch and see it's eight p.m. I bow my head to say my prayer and stand. The chatting of voices is getting louder by the window. I hear Malcom's voice talking about the bar in walking distance. I walk down the aisle and head outside. I might not drink, but I think it's time to do some male bonding here.

The cold air hits me right in the face when I open the door. Several soldiers are about a hundred feet away, migrating in a circle. Malcom is standing right at the door with his hand in a fist. I guess he was about to knock.

"Hey, man, we're headed to the bar off-base. It's about a mile down the road to Cummings. Wanna join us?" Malcom asks.

"Sure, I'll go for a bit."

All the guys start to clap. "All right, let's get this party started."

I CAN HEAR the music blasting from the road. The bar is on the end of a long strip building. The place looks to be around ten feet wide. There are about ten people standing in line to get in. There are two bouncers guarding the door checking IDs. It freezing outside, and I can see the puff of smoke coming out of my nose when I breathe out.

"You cold, Linkin?" a soldier beside me asks. "I can't feel anything on my body. The temperatures at night are brutal." We both start laughing.

I enter the bar, and there is a mixture of people all over the place. It seems a little dark for a bar, but there is a multicolored flashing light around the dance floor to the left. A DJ is set up on stage, playing a slow song. It's very busy tonight. The wooden bar straight across from us is full.

A group of girls are leaving one of the high-top tables, so we head that way to grab it. I always felt out of place in a bar, but the guys need to like me and trust me so, when they need my help, they will come to me.

Malcom heads to the bar to get us some drinks. I decide on a soft drink with cherries. I notice the women in here are barely clothed. Most of them have on a short, tight mini dress that should only be worn at home. All the women in here are gorgeous, and they know it. I look around the bar, and all I see are girls hanging off the men. I shift in my seat, feeling uncomfortable.

I'm brought out of my thoughts when Malcom sits down my drink.

"Here you go, drink up," he says with a cocky smile on his face.

I have to abide by the rules.

I see a familiar female out on the dance floor, sandwiched between two guys. The music playing now is faster and more upbeat. In a matter of minutes, the guy behind her grabs her hair, twisting it in his hand, and pulls her back, hard, against him. I see her face flinch from the pain he caused. I quickly jump off the stool and head towards the dance floor. I am talking to God in my head while I walk toward them. I have to remember not to use violence.

I reach the dance floor and head to the center where they have moved her. The closer I get, the more intensely my rage is flowing through my body. My fist is balled up beside me. I arrive next to them, and Darcy's head quickly turns toward me. I can see fear in her eyes but also anger. All of a sudden, I see her knee come up and hit the guy in the nuts, then she takes her left foot and sweeps it behind his lower legs causing him to fall backwards.

She's already on top of him and punching him in the face. All of us run over to get her off him when the other guy who was dancing with her grabs her arm. It was like a flash of lighting, so fast. She punches him behind his ear. He loses his equilibrium, tumbles backwards, and he is knocked out. I am really impressed but worried at the same time.

"Okay! That's enough. I think you proved your point to both of these guys." I say, looking at both men lying on the hard dance floor, out cold. There are lots of people circled around.

"I can handle my own," Darcy says, jumping up off the ground. She walks over to me, moving her head up to look at me. Her chest is moving in and out very fast, and her hands are twitching.

I can tell she's pissed. I don't know what has happened to her in the past, but I'm going to find out. She needs to control her temper.

AFTER A FEW minutes talking with the owner at the bar, he kicked both guys out. He did tell Darcy that if something like this happens again, she will not be allowed back in. She was not happy about it and just walked out the door. She was like a lit fuse about to blow. I decide to wait a couple of days before I confront her about what happen in my room and about the bar scene.

I finish my drink and order another. The bar is half empty now, and all of us are at the high-top table.

"Another one?" the pretty red headed waitress asks with a charming smile.

I want to say no, but I am trying to be good company with the guys. Since Darcy left, the guys and I have been talking about the football game on T.V. A few ladies strode over to make conversation, but no one seemed interested. One of the guys, Brody, left with one of them, but they said she's one of his regulars.

So, Linkin, I saw Darcy run out of your chapel earlier tonight. Can I ask what all that was about?" Malcom leans in over the table.

I sit down my drink and place both elbows on the table and lean towards him.

"Nothing happened. I was in the middle of facetime with one of my clients when I noticed she was there. She told me she wanted to check my calf out, and once she was done, she left."

"Chaplain, I think she's got the hots for you. All the guys, including me, have tried to pursue her, and she's turned us all down," Malcom admits.

"Obviously, she pines after you," Randy says as he points his beer at me. "I decided to confront her, one day, about the connection I felt with her, but all I got was a throat punch. That chick has some serious issues with men, and somehow, she's fond of you."

This isn't the first time a woman has the hots for me. But I'm dedicated to my job, and my number one goal is to give faith in God to all. There is only one person that I would change my life for, and she's not ready and probably never will be.

11

Sophia

THIS WEEK HAS been so long. My boutique has been very busy with brides and grooms. Zip flew down to help me with multiple orders. He really stepped up to help me with the inventory of the new line of fabric that came in. His boyfriend, Cruz, decided to run his shop in New York until I am done with this Godzilla bride. The girl has changed her mind several times and finally decided on an ivory lace strapless dress with a mermaid silhouette and an empire waist. The train will be a plum purple in a velvet material that will flow out in ruffles. She wants the train longer than the typical dress. There will also be a plum colored ribbon that is about two inches wide and ties in a large bow at the back.

I just walked into my place after eight hours of working on her dress. My feet ache so bad from my heels, and my hands feel so stiff from sewing and attaching fabric. I strip off my clothes while I head to the bathroom. I start the bathtub and add some Epsom salt into the water. In the bedroom, I open my top drawer to grab a long sleeve Victoria secret gown I got for Christmas last year.

I slide down in the hot bath water and stretch my legs. I sink down until the water reaches above my shoulders. I let my body relax and close my eyes. Within minutes my body is in heaven. The temperature is just right, and I start to dose off.

I'm lying in my bed; my eyes are covered with something so I can't see. My jaw hurts badly, and when I try to open my mouth, it shoots pain up to my temples. I try to move my hands up to my face, but they are wrapped in something that smells like leather. I decide to try to move my legs, but two hands grab my ankles and flip me onto my stomach. I try to scream, but I forgot my mouth would not open, and excruciating pain makes me yelp.

I start to move from side to side and push myself up to try to get away, but these large hands are pulling me back towards the end of the bed. I feel something like rope being tied around my ankles. My muscles are tensing up while whoever is tying me up finishes his job. I tremble. There's only silence. I wait, listening for any kind of sound. Maybe I can roll off the side of the bed to get to the phone across the room, on my desk.

I feel the bed shift down. Ouch! A sharp point bites into the crack of my ass. Shit. Another sharp pain pierces at the crack of my ass. Then I feel something warm near the anus. I feel something cool being rubbed there. I am now panicking. I can't move. I scream inside, "HELP." I feel hot tears running down my cheeks. I am trapped in my own bed about to be raped and killed. All of a sudden, my face is pushed down in the sheets of the bed and another hand comes around my stomach to lift my ass up. I know what is about to happen, and there is nothing I can do about it. I close my eyes and pray to God to help me.

I feel my heart beating through my chest.

I hear a male laugh. That voice sounds like Brad. He found me. He's going to kill me.

"Tonight, you die, bitch, but before you do, I will enjoy destroying your ass first," he says as he slams into me.

"Oh my god!" I cry out in pain.

I shoot up, causing the chilled water to splash over the tile floor. I place my hand over my chest to calm my beating heart. I close my eyes and do the breathing technique Linkin showed me. It doesn't take long for my heart to slow down and my breathing to get back to a normal pace.

I lift with my arms, trying to stand up, but my legs are wobbly. I wait a few minutes, and try again to stand up straight. My knees are weak, but I swing one leg over the tub while I keep a death grip on the edge. I have one leg on the floor and one still in the bath. I am sitting like a cowgirl on a saddle, but I don't care; if I stand right now, my ass is on the ground.

Ten minutes later, I am now standing on both legs. I stabilize myself and reach for the towel. I dry off and grab my sleeping gown. I grab the door knob and push open the door, but my body stands still. I look around to make sure nothing looks out of the ordinary.

Within minutes, I run toward the bed and launch myself on it. I take the covers at the end of the bed and pull them up to my breasts. I reach over to the night stand and dial the one person I know will understand my nightmare.

I wait patiently while facetime rings, showing my reflection on the screen. I look like total hell. My face has red blotches where I cried. My lip is red and raised where I bit down on it during my dream.

BOING!

"Hey!" Linkin says with a smile which then turns to a frown when he sees my appearance. "What happened?" He sits up tall in his bed.

"I...I." I can't bring myself to speak.

"Okay, tell me about your day," he asked.

"Work has been really busy this week. I had several clients in need of a special wedding dress. One of the women is a Godzilla bitch. I called Zip to come help me till I can catch up."

"Good. I'm glad Zip is there to help."

"Yes, he's been a life saver. He's got his boyfriend running his business while he's with me. If he wouldn't have showed up, I might have been on action nine news…'Crazy wedding boutique owner hits the bride in the head with her homemade bridal shoes,'" I say, biting my lip then yelping afterwards because I forgot it was sore from the first bite.

"What happened to your lip?" Linkin speaks in a hard tone, but his eyes show compassion.

"I had a bad dream in the bathtub when I fell asleep. He came back to kill me." I sob out loud and then slap my hand over my mouth, and my body just shakes.

"What happened?"

12

Linkin

IT HAS BEEN a hell of a week. I want to talk with Darcy about what happened in the room and to make sure she is doing okay. I noticed she's been very distant with everyone.

I see her wander out of the recreational center. I jog up to her and touch her arm lightly. She turns to me with a murderous look. She swears under her breath and steps back from me like I'm going to hurt her.

"What's going on, Darcy? Something happened, and you need to tell me. Did someone hurt you?" I ask.

"First, I want to apologize for touching you. I had no right to do that," she says, taking a deep breath and tilting her face up to the sky. She looks back at me with tears in her eyes.

"Let's go talk in my office, away from others' ears," I say, motioning with my arm in the direction of the chapel.

We enter the church and head down the aisle. The floor creaks while we walk. Once I step up on the stage, her hand grabs my arm. I turn to her, and she collapses in my arms, sobbing.

"Hey. Ssh… it's okay. Let's sit down right here. What's wrong, Darcy?" I sit down on the edge of the stage.

"Look, I'm sorry for crying like this. I thought I could hide all the bullshit, but after the guy pulled my hair, it triggered the anger I have been holding in."

I sit there patiently, ready to listen. I watch as she shifts a few times then rolls her shoulders back.

"I was out at a club, a year ago, with some girl-friends of mine. We were having a good time. A slow song came on, and this guy walked over and asked me to dance. He took my hand and led me out in the middle of the dance floor and wrapped me in his arms with my back to him. I thought it was a strange way to dance, but I continued to go with the flow. Then another guy came up in front of me and had me sandwiched between them. At this point, I was nervous. The new guy grabbed my hip so tight it shot a sharp pain down my leg. I tried to pull away, but both of them were too strong for me. The music changed to some kind of fast song, and they kept close so I could not get out. I yelled, but the music was too loud, and no one was paying any attention to us." She starts to stand up.

Now she is pacing back and forth right beside me. I want to tell her to take a break, but I can tell she needs to get this out.

"They danced me off the dance floor and headed us behind the DJ's stand. I decided to try to knee the guy in front of me, but when my knee went up, he moved out of the way, and the other guy grabbed my hair, covered my mouth, and dragged me out the back door. It was pitch dark outside. I guess the bar didn't believe in lightposts out back. I knew what was about to happen, and I was going to try again to get away." She sits down, folds her hands, and places them in her lap.

I know what she is about to tell me, and it makes me want to go find these two guys and tie them to a damn tree, naked, and put some mean ass swans around them to attack their dicks. I stay still, making eye contact to let her know she can continue.

"The guy behind moved out of the way while the other guy pushed my back against the brick building. I let my body relax so he would let his guard down some. The stupid guy did, and I made a fist out of my right hand and swung up and punched him behind the ear. He tumbled straight to the ground, and I took the advantage to run as fast as I could around the building. I made it around the corner, but someone grabbed the back of my hair and pulled me backwards," she says, jumping back up and pacing the stage again.

I decide to intervene now.

"How did you feel?" I ask to encourage her to open up.

"I was terrified but also pissed off. I wanted to turn back around and kick their ass. If I had a gun, I probably would have shot them," she says, lifting her hand and bringing it down to smack the podium beside her. She yelps in pain.

She looks at me briefly before she turns and sits back down on the edge of the stage. She keeps herself shifted to the side, with her face toward the long stained glass window to the left.

"Sorry about that. I get furious when I think about that night." She turns to face me for a split second with sadness in her eyes, but turns back to look at the window.

She lets out a quick huff. "The guy I knocked out had awaken. The other guy had me by the hair and was dragging me back behind the building. I kicked and hollered the whole time he tugged my body across the gravel.

"He stopped. He let go of my hair only to place his

hand to my throat. His hand was tight enough that I couldn't get any words out. The other guy walked over to where I lay and had this wide wicked grin on his face. He unzipped his pants." I can see her swallow hard.

I close my eyes and say a silent prayer to help her finish telling what happened. This is the hardest part for someone to tell, and I am here with open arms to make her feel safe afterwards if needed.

"He unzipped his pants and told the other guy to flip me over. He pushed my body flat on the ground and held me down while he rammed his penis into me," she admits with a sob.

I place my hand on her shoulder for support while she continues.

"After he got his fill of me and spilled his nasty seed in me, the other guy got his turn also. They took turns until, I guess, their dicks got raw and they didn't need my pussy no more," she says.

She now turns to me with a red face. "You know what he said? He said, 'You deserved it, you little slut.'

"They walked off, and I had no strength to move. I lay there for at least an hour before I could get up. A guy who was a bartender came out to smoke, saw me, and carried me in. The police was called."

"Did they find the guys who did this?" I ask, concerned.

I watch as she picks at her skin. It must be something she does when she's nervous. She looks up at me and something's different in her eyes. I usually can guess what my clients are thinking or feeling and what they are about to say, but with her, I can't. It must be something difficult to talk about.

She leans forward, towards me, but stops before she gets too close. "They did, but not right away. I found out a month later that I was pregnant."

Silence. I just stare at her in disbelief. These guys stole something valuable from her, and then she was faced with the unthinkable: a baby.

"How did you feel about that?" I ask.

When you talk with someone who's been raped, you have to make sure you don't push the issue.

"I was disgusted with myself."

"Why? You didn't do anything wrong. Those guys did."

"I had a meltdown when I found out I was pregnant. I fought between abortion or keeping the baby," she sighs heavily.

I knew not to speak at this point of her opening up. She needs to let this out. Whatever decision she made, it was hers and her decision only.

We sit there for a few awkward minutes. I want to let her choose what she wants to do. I can see, now, why she's always over working herself. I hear she's always exercising and keeping busy. Since I have been here, I've noticed how reserved she is. Even if she likes to joke with me and was always following me around until that night. I see where she let down that shield she puts around herself so no one gets close.

"Maybe we can talk more tomorrow. I have gotten a lot off my chest, and I thank you for listening. I apologize for the awkward moment in your room. You were the first man I felt attracted to, and safe with, since my attack." She stands, getting ready to walk out.

I place my hand on her arm. "I am your friend and your chaplain if you need me for anything. I apologize too, for not correcting you when you touched me."

"Oh, before I leave. I saw the way you look at the beautiful woman on facetime. I know that you think you are dedicated to God, but you also need to think of your happiness."

"What do you mean, how I looked at Sophia?" I say with concern. My job as a chaplain is my priority.

"When this Sophia was talking, your shoulders were lowered and relaxed. Your body had leaned toward your phone, and your eyes were completely focused on hers. At first, I just stood there, watching how attentive you were to your client, but watching your body language, I knew you were smitten. I was upset because I'd finally found someone I didn't tense around.

"This woman, she trusts you too. I can tell her tragic event is new, and she depends on your help. I can tell, one day, she will want you to save her." She jumps off the stage and runs out the door.

I shake my head. She's right about my feelings for Sophia. I walk toward my room to check and see if, maybe, I had a missed call from her. Today was our weekly facetime day. I enter my room, bend down, and grab my gym bag. I dig through my dirty, stinky clothes and grab my phone. Nothing. I head toward the dresser for my running pants. Today is the first day without snow, and it's a good run to talk with the Lord about things that are happening in these girls' lives.

13

Linkin

THE PHONE RINGS right when I head out the door. I jog back to the old wooden desk and pick up.

"Hello?"

Nothing. I can hear Sophia's voice but very faintly. The screen is all gray. I tap on it.

"Hello," I say again.

Her face pops up, blemished. I can see her eyes glisten with tears. Her face is red and splotchy like she's been crying already.

She starts to tell me about how busy work has been. Zip is still helping her with her big order. She looks really ashy, and the bottom two inches of her hair is wet. She must have just gotten out of the bath. When I look closely, there is an abrasion on her bottom lip, just like last time.

"Are you okay?"

"I must have dozed off in the bath again. The dream seemed so real. He was trying to kill me. He was so furious with me."

I notice that these nightmares happen when she's anxious. It's hard on clients when any kind of noise, smell, or even tiredness can trigger an episode. She really needs to work on finding out what can help her release those feelings she's keeping to herself.

"Sophia, have you written in your journal?"

"Well," she said, looking over toward something in her room, "I did write a little."

"That's great. Read it to me?" I ask.

She hesitates for a moment, but she reaches over the side of the bed and grabs a yellow book covered in flower designs. She holds the book to her chest and sighs. She slides back to the headboard and situates the phone so I can read it.

"I don't want to read it out loud, so I will let you read it, but I couldn't write about my feelings on if I feel like I deserve what happened," she whispers.

"Hey, you're taking a step forward just writing in a journal. So, let me read what you wrote." This is a big step forward; I'm so proud of her.

Slowly, she shifts the phone where I can see the first page. The page is golden yellow with a daisy flower up in the right upper corner. She's written in black cursive. Her hand writing is very elegant. I start from the beginning.

Dear Diary,

I was told to just write down my day. How I was feeling. That it may help me. So here it goes. Today is Sunday. I rode by Brad's parents' house today. They have been calling me every day since the horrific events. It's not their fault what he did to me, but I am so angry. His court date is coming up soon; my lawyer called to notify me that I will have to testify. I pulled in their driveway and put the gear shift in park. I cut off the engine and just sat there, mentally preparing myself to get out. Eventually, I decided I am not ready to talk with them, and I'm not sure I will ever be. I turned the car back on and pulled out of the driveway. My phone began to ring. I know it's her, his mother, but I keep driving. She left me a voicemail. I hit to listen, and it comes on my blue tooth.

"Sophia. Turn back around, honey. We are so sorry what Brad did to you. Paul and I understand that you are scared, angry, and confused. We love you, and if you need anything from us, we are just a phone call away."

I drove till it was dark. After several hours, I asked Siri on my phone for the closest hotel and headed in that direction. I pulled in the parking lot. My head felt like someone was stabbing me with a hot poker stick. My chest was tight, and I couldn't get a good breath. I closed my eyelids and leaned my head back on the head rest. And I prayed. I asked God to forgive me for my sins and to help me. I have lost my faith in him. I yelled in my head, "Why God, why? What did I do to deserve this? How could you let this man brutally cut my body in pieces, rape me, and beat me till he thought I was dead. What god does this?"

That night, I lay my head down on the pillow at the hotel, and that was the first time I slept all night. I have a lot of healing to do, and my heart is one of them.

I am so proud of her. It takes courage to do what she did. I believe that we are on the right track for recovery. Some of my guard friends have checked in on Brad, and some inmates are pissed at what he did. The gossip has traveled around the detention center where he is being held until his court appearance. He's been isolated from the others. I received an email from the officer on duty about the upcoming legal matters for the client but also about an article on the subject. I hate to bring it up, but Sophia already knows about the upcoming court case.

"I received an email for the officer a few days ago.

Did you happen to see the article that was posted in the Charlotte Observer?" I ask.

Her body stiffens. "Do I want to read it? I know they put things in there that happened to me, and now the whole world knows."

"Yes, it does. And you know everything that's happened to you. I want you to read it and write down how you are feeling in your journal. This is the second step to moving on, Sophia. Maybe after reading the article, it will give you some relief to know what is going to happen to him," I admit.

Wide-eyed, she sits there and just stares at her journal. Her sad-watery eyes gaze at mine in the phone. "Okay, I'll try," she says and swallows hard.

I have noticed she does this a lot when she's trying to calm herself down. It can be a body movement people do when they're nervous or afraid.

She gives me a weak smile. "Bye, Linkin," she says, and the screen goes blank.

I place my phone back down on the desk and decide a long run would be good for me. I can talk with God and release some frustration I am holding on to.

I head out the door and put on an orange face mask with reflectors, so if I come in contact with anyone in the woods, they will know it's just me and not an animal. I begin my jog. The wind is strong tonight. I grab my scarf and place it in the hole of my jacket so the cold air won't get in. I was told that when the wind is below zero, the movement of your body running can increase the air movement coming in contact with your body.

Half way up the trail, I see the shadow of someone running up ahead. I keep running, one foot in front of the other. When I run I feel like a brand-new person. Losing myself in my thoughts, I think about my life. What I have accomplished since I chose the military chaplain life for a career. I love what I do. What better way to spread God's word then helping U.S. soldiers with spiritual support and ordinary comfort?

Then came the assignment, Sophia, who was brutally beaten and raped by her military boyfriend. I have counseled young men and women who come home from the stress of the army, who push their anger out on a family member, but this case is different. I was called by the client's girlfriend's mother for help. But my duty is to serve the Lord, and if helping this young woman get past her fear of the tragic event is where he sent me, that is what I will do.

I am now feeling the adrenaline pumping after running for over half an hour. I slow my pace to a fast walk since I am now inching up a hill. I see something yellow a little off the trail. It's the shadow I saw earlier. My lungs are still screaming for air, but it's not as drastic as when I was in full jog. I come up to the log where the yellow shadow is sitting. Darcy is resting there with her arms wrapped around her legs. I stop in front of her. She looks up, and all I can see of her is her eyes. She has her yellow face mask on, but I can tell she's been crying.

"Can I sit?" I ask.

She scoots over to the right a little, giving me some room to sit down.

I take the open spot, twist so I am facing her, and wait. She's fumbling with her hands, and I can tell that she is about to open up, and what she's about to tell me is going to be a huge relief off her chest. I could tell, from the first day I met her, that she hides her stress but took her anger out on everyone else. That's why the guys call her the tough one.

"I couldn't kill it," she whispers. "I hated that I was pregnant by one of the two rapists. I tried to induce a miscarriage, but I could not force my hand to ram the metal coat hanger I took out of my closet up my vagina. I watched a movie, one time, where a woman did that out of revenge on her husband for cheating, and she lost the baby, but I couldn't do it," she sobs. Her whole body is shaking now. She starts rocking back and forth on the log, her hands still wrapped around her legs.

"How does that make you feel?"

"Pissed. I want those assholes found and charged

for their wrong. You know that when they finally found them, there wasn't enough evidence, and they were let go?" She takes a deep breath before continuing. "Hurt. When I look in my baby girl's eyes, all I see is anger that they did this to me. What am I suppose to say to her when she grows up and asks about her father? Do I tell her what happened and that one of them is her father? I have so much rage inside me I am about to explode. I just got back from maternity leave after having her. I wanted to come back to work. My mother has her until I am able to go home."

"I'm sorry," I whisper and place my hand on her upper arm.

Lord, if you can hear me, I need your help. This is a lot on this girl's plate. I need any guidance you can give me to help her. She needs to heal herself inside from the damage that has been done by those guys.

"One morning, I decided to head to the abortion clinic to rid myself of this bastard child." She laughs, but it sounds more like a sob. "I pulled up, and there was a preacher with a speaker phone, holding a bible in front of the clinic. He was talking about the bible verses and how God says not to kill. You know what he said to me when I walked up to the door? He got me good on this one. He said, 'Psalm 127:3, Behold, children are a gift from god. The fruit of the womb is a reward.'"

"It had nothing to do with you, Darcy. He was out there, spreading the word of God. He did not know you had been raped," I say.

"Well, he knew after I took the microphone and told everyone about that night. You know what he said?" She looks at me, and her lips tremble.

"What?"

"Nothing. He said nothing. He wrapped his arms around me and told me everything will be okay. God has a plan."

What do I say to this? This man was right and wrong in what he did. A person has to make the right decision on their own.

"My little girl was conceived from rape but a gift from God. She completes me. Does that sound strange? My anger is due to the fact that the rapists are still out there, and I want them to pay. I need to let this anger go, for me, for my daughter, and for my job. It's affecting my life."

"There's nothing wrong with what you feel. You were raped by sick men, and I believe, one way or another, they will pay for their sins," I say.

I lift myself off the log and turn to Darcy. I hold my hand out for her to grab. She places her delicate, ice-cold hand in mine. I pull her up off the log.

"Let's finish our jog and head back for some hot

coco with large marshmallows." I turn and start running up the hill.

I hear the crunching of Darcy's boots on the frosty leaves on the dirt. The sound is getting closer, and I know she is about to pass me. I can feel my hot breath on the face mask as I inhale slowly to regulate my breathing while I run.

I slow down when, all of a sudden, I hear something move in the woods. In Alaska, you have to be very careful what you run into. I don't carry a gun on me, but I saw Darcy had one strapped to her calf. I reach out and tap her arm. She turns to me, and I can only see the shadow of her face, but I can see the white of her eyes from the large moon above.

I whisper, "Something is moving to my right. The noise is too loud to be a small animal. So, I need you to grab your gun for safety. I hear moose are mean."

She lets out a giggle. "Chaplain Linkin, a moose is not going to be out here in the dark. Now a deer, wolf, or any other creature is a different story. She shakes her head but reaches down, snaps the strap, and pulls out the gun.

We walk in silence for about five hundred feet until we reach slosh mud from so much snow. I hear trickling drop sounds off in the distance.

"Let's go see the creek," Darcy says. She bends down to place her gun back in her holster.

I go off the trail first, and Darcy follows. Rain mixed with snow starts to fall heavily, and a huge gust of wind hits my body and slithers down my face and neck. I continue down the hill, holding on to small trees for support.

"The sound is getting closer. I hear a whistling, but it's not the wind," Darcy says.

As I listen, I hear crackling sounds. I continue to walk down the hill, and wet snow slush brushes up my boot, to my pants.

"It must be chunks of ice. Look there," I say as I point at the dip in the ground where a reflection of ice chunks in the creek show in the light of the bright moon above.

"Look," she points at the icebergs crashing against each other while water shoots up between the cracks.

I look and see a deer on the other side of the creek. We stand there and watch as it grazes on some kind of seeds laying in the snow.

"Be very quiet. Take a seat, and rest a little on that large fallen tree then we will head back." I walk over and take a seat.

Darcy follows.

"Can I ask you a question, Linkin? Don't think like a preacher but as a man," she says in a whisper, making sure the deer can't hear her, but it raises its head anyway and runs off.

"Oops. Sorry," she says.

"So, what's your question?" I ask.

"The woman you were talking to, is she a client of yours? She is very attentive to you when you are trying to calm her down. I overheard you talking to her like a counselor but also talking to her like you know her other than that," she says, and I can hear the curiosity in her voice.

"I was called to come pray over her after a horrific event that happened to her. Her mother talked me into pretending I was getting married."

"Why would you pretend to be married when you are a chaplain and was called to pray for her?" Darcy asks.

"Sophia's mother thought it was best to pretend I was getting married. See, Sophia owns a little boutique and does wedding wardrobes. Her passion is to find the perfect wedding dress and help the groom find his perfect suit."

"So, let me get this straight. The mother wants you to pretend to get married so you can help her daughter recover by pretending to dress you up for a wedding? That is so screwed up." Darcy stands up and crosses her arms. "I would be pissed. If my mother would have pulled something like that with me, I would have cut all ties with her."

"A mother's love is unconditional, and she will go

to all ends to help her child. She thought that getting her involved in a fake wedding will help keep her mind off the awful things she's been through by giving her an assignment. That is the only reason why I agreed to it. I prayed, after agreeing to it, and asked the Father to help me make the right decision," I say, standing up and looking out at the glorious creek.

The moon is shining down through the snow-covered leaves of the forest trees, and I close my eyes and just take a moment of peace. The moment is interrupted when a cell begins to ring. I reach down for my phone but realize I left it on the desk in my room. Looking at Darcy, she reaches in her coat pocket and pulls out her phone.

"Yes, Sargent," she replies. "Okay, sir, we are on our way back. Sir, I have Chaplain Linkin with me. We took a run into the mountains and found a creek and stopped to rest. On our way, sir." Darcy hits the end button and tucks her phone back in her jacket.

She looks at me.

"Missiles have been launched from Korea for practice. Sargent Ayers needs everyone prepared in case they decide it's more than practice shots."

This is not a good sign.

I do a couple of stretches before my run back to camp. Darcy and I start back up the hill to get to the dirt path. We both stay silent during our way back.

We know what can happen if a missile is sent our way, and we have to be prepared to fight. I was trained as a soldier before pursuing the ministry life. I am not against fighting for my country with a gun if it's saving God's children.

After thirty minutes of intense running we have made it back to camp. The base is filled with military fighter planes, combat tanks, and the underground bunker has been opened and is getting prepared for launch if needed.

I go back to the chapel to get changed. I see three missed calls from Sophia. I dial the number, but before the first ring, I hear an air-raid siren wail outside. I hit end on my call and place my cell in my cargo pocket on the side of my pants. I head outside, and up in the dark sky, a huge fire ball comes descending down toward the center of camp. I see Malcom and Brody drop and roll under a combat tank to take cover.

Out of the corner of my eye, I see Darcy running toward the underground bunker. It's like watching things in slow motion. The roar of flame crashes into the two-story training building and about one hundred feet from Darcy. I see her body bounce up in the air and hit the ground hard. I run very quickly toward her, but the hit of the missile made a crater in the ground. I jump down on the side and slide down the rubble. At the bottom, I see her lying there with her back flat against the ground and her eyes closed. I get to her and get down on my knees. I place my fingers against her carotid and check for a pulse. It's faint but there. I need her to live. Darcy's too young to die, and her little precious angel at home needs her. I bow my head and pray.

Our Father, I pray you will lay your healing hands on Darcy. I pray you take away her pain and hold her in your healing wings and make her whole again.

My other hand that was placed on her chest starts to move up and down with more force. I lift my head, and when I open my eyes, she's looking right at me. She tries to speak but whimpers. Time becomes crucial for Darcy. I need to get her out of here and to a clinic. I watch as more fire balls fly through the air and hit off, more toward the mountains.

"Darcy, I am crawling up to see if I can get some help. I will need help just in case your neck broke or you have internal injuries. I don't want to risk dragging you out myself," I say, backing up and turning to crawl up to the top.

I get to the top and peek out. The scene is unreal. A heavy smoke floats all around me. I see two soldiers near me, lying on the ground. I look over to the right, where Malcom and Brody lie, still under the tank, unharmed. Malcom is hollering towards me, but I can't quite figure out what he is trying to say.

Think. Think. Think.

I decide to do the army crawl towards the guys. As I slide my body across the sand, I feel a sharp pain on my torso where my shirt drifted up with the friction of sliding in the dirt. I continue to move until I reach my destination.

"Man, are you okay?" Brody says, grabbing the back of my shirt and sliding me under the tank with them.

"Yes. I'm fine other than the whole front of my torso feeling like it is on fire. I must have gone over glass or something while moving on the ground to get here," I say. "But we need to get back to Darcy. She's hurt pretty badly."

"I saw her fly up in the air. She hit the ground hard," Malcom says, shaking his head. "Let's go get our girl."

I look over at Malcom and see concern in his eyes. I have a good hunch he's saying this more for him. I can see the way he watches her around camp. He takes small glimpses at her when we all sit down for meals. Darcy needs a good man, and in the little time I have known him, Malcom seems genuine.

Malcom rolls out first and rises up to look around.

He squats down, "Okay, I think we are safe to stand."

We slide out and stand. I glance around then start

to walk one step at time. I can hear the guys' footsteps behind me as we head toward Darcy. I hope she's still alive.

When we reach the large hole in the ground from the impact of a missile, I sit in the dirt and slide down the rubble to were Darcy lies. The ashy smell of smoke from the fire singes my nose.

"Watch out," Malcom hollers.

I get down and crawl over to Darcy and cover her body with mine.

My chest tightens at the sounds of gunfire back and forth. I need to get her out of here and checked on. Her pulse is weak, and her breath has slowed down to ten per minute.

"All right, let's get her out of here," I say, signaling the guys to come over to help me lift her. "We don't know how serious her injuries are, so I need Brody to stand in front of her, facing her head. I need you to slide your palms under her upper back and stop at the shoulder blades."

"Okay, Linkin." He secures his palms underneath her.

"Brody, when Malcom and I lift her body, I need you to secure her neck with your forearms so it stays straight," I command.

Malcom moves closer. "Okay, so, where do I need to be?"

"I want you in the middle. I need your arms to go under her mid back and under her butt. I will take her legs and keep them straight. We will go slowly since we don't know her injuries."

Once they have situated themselves, we start to walk at a faster pace toward the clinic. We stand at the closed door, and Brody uses one of his feet to kick backward at it. Nothing happens. He tries one more time, and the door finally opens, and we enter. We move through the front office to the back.

"There. Right there is the exam room," Malcom says.

We shuffle to room one and carefully lay her body down on the white table. Malcom and Brody leave to go find the doctor while I stay and watch over her. I walk over to the cabinet and grab a rag. I turn on the sink and let the water warm up.

I press the warm cloth on her face gently to get the caked-up dirt off. I hear commotion in the hall. My gut twists with nerves watching Darcy's pale body.

"We found the doctor."

The older man comes in, clothes torn and face caked with dirt. He comes over and pulls out his stethoscope to listen to her chest. He starts tapping her abdomen all over.

"She needs to be taken to the hospital for x-rays. Her lungs are clear, and her apical heart rate is sixty beats a minute. The liver and spleen are swollen. I will know more after several more tests," he says while scribbling down stuff on the notepad on the counter.

Darcy is being transferred to the hospital, and I will head up there to check on her later after I am looked at.

I ask the doctor to also look at my torso. He lifts my shirt up.

"Son, I see a lot of metal and glass particles protruding out of your skin. I need you to take your shirt off and lie down," he orders and heads over to the cupboard to grab a bottle of stuff. He then reaches into a glass canister and grabs several Q-tips.

A cold spray hits my chest and my instinct is to rise up. "That is cold," I say.

"That's an antiseptic spray before I start picking out the objects out of your skin. I can't numb you up, so it's going to be painful." He reaches for a blue package with metal instruments in it.

AFTER AN HOUR of pure torture and two shots, I am on my way back to the chapel. The doctor talked to me the whole time, telling me what was happening. For some reason, Korea decided to test out one of their missiles, and it ended up hitting our camp. A call was made, and angry words were said. Several snipers were hidden in the mountains, ready to shoot if we fought back. The president's been called here to talk, and now, this matter lies in his hands.

Finally in my room, I sit down on the bed and gaze out the window. Rain and sleet hits the glass, making a noise like little dancers tapping away on the floor. I lie back on the bed and close my eyes. I wonder if Sophia has seen the news. I would really like to hear her voice. I am startled when my phone rings.

"Hello," I say in a groggy voice.

"Linkin. Are you okay?" Sophia asks.

I stretch a little and scoot myself up, leaning on the headboard. "Yes. I'm fine." *Well that's weird. I was just thinking of her calling me.*

Shit, I need to get a grip.

"It's all over the news; a missile hit. I have been calling you for two hours. I was so worried." Her words come out wobbly.

I smile. Just those little words, that she was worried about me, make me tingle with joy. My mom always said that, one day, when the right one comes along, she will knock me off my feet. When I was taking my classes for ministry, I was taught about celibacy. All men and woman lust over one another, but when you question your celibacy for a woman, then you decide what path you want to take.

"Mom and I were looking up some fabric for a client when a news alert came on, saying Korea fired a missile for practice, and then they showed pictures of gunfire being exchanged.”

“I’m okay, Darcy. one of the soldiers, was thrown up in the air when a small missile hit the ground, but she’s alive. The smoke covered the whole camp from the missile hitting,” I say, now struggling to breathe.

“Oh. Good. I am glad she is okay.”

There is a long moment of silence, and I can barely hold my eyes open. I am so exhausted. I am about to tell her I’ll call her later, but she interrupts me.

“I miss you, Linkin,” she says, her voice sounding hopeful. “I really like talking to you. You make me feel safe.”

I wish I could see her beautiful face. “I miss you too, Sophia. I am not sure how long I will be here, but when I get home, I would like to take you out. Not as a date but a good friend outing,” I say with a smile.

She’s not ready for a date.

“Oh, I received an email today notifying me about Brad’s court. It’s next week.” She sounds worried.

“Before you go, I want you to facetime me, and we will talk. I will pray with you.”

Her eyes fill with tears, and her lip trembles. I know how scared she is to see Brad after what happened. I just want to put my arms around her and just hold her tight. I can’t fight these feelings, taking over me, any longer. Sophia is my choice.

"Sophia. Don't cry. You are going to feel such a relief when you show up in court and show Brad you are okay. You are going to show him how strong you are and that what he did was wrong," I say with encouragement.

Her lip stops trembling, and a soft smile appears. A bubble deep down in my stomach appears with her smile. How can that be?

14

Sophia

As I STAND inside mother's living room, I consider calling Linkin back. The emotions that have been running through my head have me freaking out a little. It's been eight months since the horrific night. Between Linkin and journaling, I am ready to forgive Brad. I pray every night that the Lord gives me strength to do what's right. I know that time heals. I know that it's normal to feel helpless, self-blame, and anger, but I want my life back. I've decided to go see Brad before the hearing just to let him know I forgive him.

I leave the living room and head to my room. I walk over to my bed and grab the computer. I let out a sigh as I open up the top and turn it on. I pull up my email and sent a message to my lawyer, letting him know to set up a time to talk to Brad.

I grab my journal and jolt down how I feel.

Dear Journal,

Soon, my worst nightmare will come true. I'm heading to see Brad for the first time since that day. I'm scared. As hard as it will be, this is something I need to do to move on. I've been praying more lately. I realized that life is short, and it is time to not let evil win.

Linkin has been my savior. I have thought over and over again about how he just squeezed into my life. I was lost after the horrific night and didn't think I could bounce back, but I did, and it's all because of him. He is my hero.

I place my journal under the mattress. I lay my head down and close my eyes. I still can't sleep at night. When I do lie down, the same nightmare awaits me in my dreams. I've been holding off taking the sleeping pills prescribed by my doctor, but tonight I think I will try it. I need to get some rest before going to see Brad.

There is a knock at my door. It creaks open slowly, and mom peeks her head in.

"Hey, honey, I came to check on you and bring you some sweet tea with blondie cookies," she says, placing them down on the bed.

When she takes a look at me her eyes widen. "Sophia, you're so pale. Please, take a sleeping pill tonight. You have to get some rest."

"Mom, I will. Do you think you can stay in here tonight and make sure I don't do anything in my sleep?" I ask.

She walks over to my dresser, takes one of the pills out, and hands it to me. She crawls in bed beside me and turns on *The Outlander.*

I AWAKEN TO sun shining through the window. I roll over and grab my cell phone to see what time it is. Wow, it's ten a.m. I slept a total of eight hours. Even though I still don't want to take medication to help me sleep, I think I'll stick with it for a bit if it helps.

I inch up off the bed and turn to check on mom, but she's not in the bed and her side is made up. I walk over to my computer and turn it on. My email shows a response from my lawyer. I click on it and read what he says. I stand there, looking at my appointment that is set for in two days. I close the laptop and go to my closet to put on some clothes. I walk into the bathroom and brush my teeth and pull my hair up in a ponytail, trying not to second guess my decision.

I take a good look at my appearance in the mirror, and my face now has color. The red blood vessels have gone out of my eyes. I am amazed at looking so much better after just getting a good night's sleep. Eyeing the left-over sugar cookies on the nightstand, I walk over and place one in my mouth. I open my door and head downstairs to see what my mother is up to.

"What are you doing?" I ask, walking into the kitchen and taking a seat at the table.

She walks over to me and takes a seat beside me. She places a newspaper down in front of me. In huge black letters on the front, it says, "Breaking News: Fort Benson, Alaska has been hit with missiles." Underneath the title is a description of what happened and then a large photo under it. I see three men carrying a soldier into a brick building. I look closer and see the white collar around one of the guys's neck. I take a closer look, trying to make out the face from the bad photograph, and it's him. It's my Linkin. *Oh my god! Where did my Linkin come from?*

I grab my phone that lay on the table and dial his number. After two rings, he picks up.

"Sophia, are you okay?" he asks, breathless.

"Yes, I am fine. Are you fine? I saw the newspaper. That was you, at the end, holding the soldier's legs, wasn't it?" I blabber out.

"It was. That's Darcy, the injured soldier I told you about. She landed really hard on the ground. She's pretty beat up. I was actually about to take an hour nap then head up to the hospital to check on her," he says, rubbing his forehead.

This Darcy must be the blond woman who stood in his room while we were facetiming one night. I notice a twitch above her right eye, and she folded her arms. She didn't look happy he was talking with me. I blew the tension of her mood off because soldiers can be moody a lot, but what if there was more to it?

"You go rest. I just saw the picture and wanted to talk to you to make sure you were okay. I'll talk to you later," I say and hang up.

I am usually not the jealous type, but to see the look of concern on his face when he talked about Darcy just hit a nerve.

"Honey, are you okay? Did something happen to Linkin?" my mom asks full of questions.

"No, he is fine, just exhausted. One of the soldiers was injured, and that was him helping carry her to safety." I start to pace back and forth.

Should I call him back. I can't believe I hung up on him, and why is he not calling me back?

"Oh, Sophia, honey, what's wrong? He is okay. Is there something you want to talk about?" mom asks, reaching over and placing her hand on top of mine.

"Mom, I'm fine." I remove my hand from under hers.

I quickly stand up and place the chair back under

the table.

"I am going to the shop. I had some new dresses come in, and I need to get them on the mannequins," I say with a weak smile.

Once I get in my car, I head to the coffee shop to get a large cold brew and a blueberry muffin. The drive is too quiet for me, so I turn on the radio to ninety-six point nine country station. A Billy Ray Cyrus song comes on: *Achy Breaky Heart*. I start to laugh but then sing out the lyrics. I put my hand to my heart when he gets to the part where he says, "don't break my heart." I love this song.

I pull up behind my boutique. I see Zip in the window, placing the new dresses on the mannequins. He has been my life saver these past couple of weeks. I am so thankful for his help.

I walk over to the window and tap on the glass. He looks over at me, a huge grin on his face. He knows he's been caught.

"What are you doing here? This is your day off to go enjoy the big city before going home," I say with both hands on my hips.

"I wanted to surprise you. Now that I have finished, I am off to look at all the hot sexy men in suits," he says wiggling his eyebrows.

He's such a pig.

I interlock our arms together and lead him out the

door. "Love you, Zip. Thank you for everything. Now, shoo, and have fun," I say, giving him a light push and closing the door behind him.

Two hours later, two brides walk in with their bridesmaids. They are best friends and want a double wedding. One girl wants to wear a cream illusion-lace halter-sheath dress with a teal green bow around the waist. The other wants the same dress but in white and with the same matching bow.

There's a total of six bridesmaids and grooms. They decide on them matching the bride and groom's teal colors. So, the men will have dark and light teal vests, the same as the girls' dresses. The grooms decide on one cream vest with swirl designs and the other, a teal vest with cream swirls. I write down everything and will be searching for the fabrics.

The chime on the door rings, bringing my attention towards the entrance. When I come around the corner, there stands Marybeth, Linkin's fake fiancée, holding a bag that says Mary's café on it.

"I come with a peace offering. Linkin called me to come check on you, and I didn't get to apologize," she says, reaching out to hand me the bag.

"Why did he want you to come check on me?" I ask, crossing my arms.

"He said that when he talked to you, he could tell something was bothering you and that you hung up on him," she says, copying me and crossing her arms.

"I had a jealous moment. You know, all women do, but I am good now. I'll call him later. Now, let's go eat and get to know one another," I say, walking back to the office and grabbing two chairs before heading back out.

"I'll go first," Marybeth offers. "My husband's name is Dean. He is Linkin's best friend. That's how I became part of the fake wedding. Dean talked him into going along with it. Your mother was a mess, and she really believed that Linkin could help you, save you from destruction." She grabs a fried green tomato and takes a bite out of it. "God always has a plan, even when you think it's not the right one."

"Well, I guess you know what happened to me," I say.

She puts her fork down on her plate.

She meets me eye to eye. "Of course. But don't be mad at Linkin. He didn't tell me; Dean did. The moment I found out about what happened and the way Linkin talked about you and saw the concern in his eyes, I knew you needed him." She held up her hand quickly, telling me she's not done.

"Do you believe in fate, Sophia?" she asks.

"Not sure. Maybe. I have a feeling you're talking about Linkin being brought into my life by fate. I don't believe God would be so cruel as to let a man rape me, abuse me, and leave me for dead. But I know that this horrific event brought Linkin and me to cross paths. He is my hero," I admit to her and myself.

He is my hero, and I make the decision, right then, to let him know.

We finish up our meals in silence. The chime of the door has us both turning around. A tall, skinny attractive man walks in. He takes off his glasses, and his eyes sparkle. They are so blue. He lifts his hand and blows a kiss our way. Okay, now things are getting weird.

"How are these two beautiful women doing today? Can I offer you two a night cap at my condo, and we can test out the bear fur in front of my fireplace?" he asks.

I stand and walk towards him ready to kick him out of my store when Marybeth's hand grabs my arm.

"Dean. Don't be an ass," she says but giggles.

So, this is her husband.

She walks over to him, lifts herself up on her toes, and gives him a big smooch. He picks her up and squeezes her so tight. I hope, one day, I can have that.

"So, this is Sophia." He walks over and wraps me in a big hug. He just holds me for a minute. He pulls away but still holds both hands on my arms. "I'm so sorry for what happened to you. When Linkin called to tell me what happened and what your mother asked from him, I knew he would not be able to live with himself if he walked away." He looks into my eyes for a moment before breaking the spell. "Well, enough with the serious stuff. Let's get down to the nitty and gritty," he says, letting go of my arms and walking over to our food.

He picks up a fried green tomato and puts the whole thing in his mouth. He starts to chew with his mouth open.

Marybeth walks up and slaps him in the back of his head.

We all start to laugh.

ON THE WAY home, my phone rings. I hit the Bluetooth button, and loud noise comes out of the speaker. "Hello?"

"Sophia," Linkin says, but my name comes out like an echo.

"The phone is staticky. Where are you?" I ask.

"I am at the airport, on the way home. Everyone is being sent home since the missile incident. They have investigators coming to look over the camp and in the trails of the mountains." His voice is coming out more clearly now.

"That was fast. I just spoke to you a few hours ago," I say, turning my blinker on to turn on my street.

"You want to tell me why you hung up on me? I was still talking to you when the phone went blank," he asks with concern.

"Well, I did. I was jealous of this Darcy woman," I say, waiting to see what he is about to say.

"You're jealous I went to help her? Do you know what this woman has been through? My job is to help everyone, not just you," he shouts in the phone.

I pull in the drive and put the shift in park. How dare he holler at me? I was just being honest. He must have feelings for her since he is so eager to snap at me asking about her.

I quickly hit end on my Bluetooth. I just hung up on him again. But he deserved it. Placing both hands on the steering wheel, I pull myself up closer and place my head on the air bag in the center. Shit, I love him.

15

Linkin

"MILK," THE BABY monitor screams out.

"Milk," baby Emma screams again.

From the moment I decided to stay and help Darcy out until she recovers from her injuries, this precious girl stole, my heart.

After being hung up on for the second time, I decided to go check on Darcy. The doctor was releasing her, but with us all being sent home from duty, she needed someone to help with Emma. Darcy's injuries are severe. She's broken her pelvis, three ribs, and has a cracked clavicle. There was no way she could take care of a thirteen-month-old baby by herself on top of her injuries.

So here I am in Raleigh, NC, staying with Darcy for a month until the doctor clears her. Sophia has called me several times, but I just hit decline. I know I need to talk to her and tell her how I feel, but Emma needs me more.

I've seen the headlines that Brad will be serving twenty-two years in jail. Dean called me right after the hearing to tell me how good Sophia did. Marybeth and her have become really close friends, and I think it's great. Sophia didn't really have anyone to talk to except her mother and I. Dean keeps me informed with her recovery and let me know that her nightmares have stopped.

Right after I landed, I called the correction center where Brad was being held. One of my clients let me know that Sophia showed up there, and she talked with Brad. After I freaked out, I called Dean and he told me Marybeth went with her, and she did really good. She told Brad she forgives him and that she was ready to move on.

"Milk. Milk. Milk..." Emma cries out.

She's mad now. I can hear her jumping up and down in her crib. This child has a temper when she doesn't get her milk after she wakes up.

I roll out of bed, heading down the hall to her room. I peek in, and she sees me and smiles. She holds her hands out.

"Lin. Milk," she says, her arms flailing up in the air.

"Hey, sweet princess. Let's go get some milk then

eat some waffles," I say, lifting her out of the crib.

I enter the kitchen and see a note is on the table. I place Emma in her high chair and walk over to the fridge to grab her milk. Walking back over to the table, I give it to her. I grab the paper and read it on the way to get some coffee.

Hey, man, I picked up Darcy to take her to PT. Fingers crossed they discharge her today, and you can go home. Malcom.

That man has it bad. Since she's been hurt, he comes two days a week to take her to physical therapy. He said that's what soldiers do for one another, but he uses that as an excuse. Darcy, on the other hand, milks up all the attention she gets. She went from a single mom to having two male dad figures in her baby's life. I just found out, two days ago, that I have been chosen as the godfather, and if anything happens to Darcy, I get Emma. But that's something I don't want to think about. I hope that Malcom steps up and admits his feelings for her.

Monday will be my last day here then I am heading back home to Virginia Beach. My neighbor, Simon, has been taking care of Max. I can't wait to see the big guy.

The uncontrollable urge to just head to Charlotte to see Sophia is too much. I miss seeing her on my phone. I miss her voice. Yet I'm being an ass for not calling her. Darcy sat down with me, the other night, and told me straight up that, sometimes in life, you must choose which dirt road to take. Sometimes you need to take the long one.

"Milk. Lin." Emma points from the high chair.

I grab her up and head down the hall to get her cleaned up and changed.

I hear a click-clack noise down the hall. I guess Darcy is back from physical therapy.

"Hey, momma's little angel," she says, walking into the room.

Emma's whole body is dancing happily. I finish dressing her in a pillow dress made out of Darcy's soldier shirt. Malcom had it made two weeks ago. It was the shirt she wore when the missile hit.

"Where is Malcom?" I ask.

"He went home to pack. I was cleared from PT, but I still have to watch my weight limit. Since this chunky monkey weights twenty-two pounds, I will still need help with her," she says, playing with Emma's hair.

"You know what? I'll fly to Virginia Beach, get Max, and drive back with my truck. I can stay a couple more weeks." I place Emma on the ground, and she grabs her momma's hand.

"NO! I mean, I would love to have you here, but you need to get home, get Max, and head to Charlotte," she says, not making eye contact.

"What did you do? Have you been talking with Marybeth? You two need to stop trying to play match maker."

She sticks her tongue out at me, turns, and walks out of the room. I need to call Dean and see what these two girls are up too, but right now, I go finish up cleaning the kitchen.

A car door shuts, and several voices come from the side of the house. That's weird because Darcy's parents left for Scotland for six months then to Paris. Since Darcy is doing fine and Malcom has decided to help her, they plan to only come home for the Holidays. I still need to talk with him about whatever they have going on. I have to make sure Emma is taken care of, and he knows she comes with the package.

The voices get closer, and Darcy walks in the kitchen with a smirk on her face. Emma follows behind her, waddling like a duck.

"What's going on?" I ask.

"You'll see," she says with a smile, and then there's a tap on the door.

She walks over, unlocks the dead bolt, and opens the door.

Marybeth comes in and swoops her in a big hug. "Finally, I get to meet you in person."

Before I can ask any questions, I see Sophia. She

steps in and looks at me then at Darcy. I feel a hand touch mine and look down to see Emma looking up at me.

"Lin. Milk," she says.

I turn to Sophia, and her eyes are glazed over with tears.

She runs out the door.

"What the hell, Sophia," Dean says as he catches himself by grabbing a hold of the door frame.

I let go of Emma's hand and run out the door after Sophia. I continue down the steps and look around, but I don't see her anywhere. I turn and head straight across the street where the walking park is located. Since it's Saturday, the field is full of children practicing soccer. I catch a glimpse of someone mooching around the brick fountain. It's Sophia; I can tell by her yellow sundress.

The whole time I'm walking over to where she sits facing the children, I have an inner discussion in my head. I was over the moon to see her beautiful face again, but also, I have to sit down and talk to her about Darcy.

I have come to the conclusion that I'd have to be straight with her. Lay it all out there for her and pray she doesn't walk away. I get to where she sits, and I just stand there, watching her observe the children playing. She's been through so much this year. I see her stand, turn, and her eyes catch mine. She's crying. Her eyes are red and swollen.

We both stand there, not moving, just staring at each other. I want to just walk right over and take her in my arms, but it's up to her to make a move. I need to know what she's thinking and what she wants.

"Are you with her? Is that her little girl in there? You two playing house with one another?" she asks.

I step closer, but not too close. "No, we are not playing house. The doctor told me what she was facing after being released. There is no way she could take care of her baby with her injuries, and her parents are older and had a hard time taking care of Emma while she was in Alaska. So, Malcom and I decided to help her."

"Who's Malcom?" she questions.

"He was one of the soldiers in the photo. He helped me get Darcy out. They both have feelings for each other but are too scared to admit it," I say.

"Oh," she says and just stands there, looking at me with those sad eyes.

"I have been chosen to be Emma's godparent. If something ever happens to Darcy, I will get her. Darcy's parents love their granddaughter, but they are done with raising children, and they are off seeing the world now," I say, waiting for her response.

She walks over to me. We are both standing there,

so close, watching one another. I can see in her eyes that she is contemplating what to say. My body is drawn to her, and I just want to reach out and wrap her in my arms.

I feel her hand grab mine. I look down at her lacing our fingers together. The excitement of her touch is new. I have never had this feeling, but I have to remember I took an oath to love God and spread his word. Celibacy is what we choose when we become a chaplain. But this magnetic feeling I have for Sophia seems right. I want this. I want her.

I decide, before anything else is said, I am going to kiss her. I wrap my arm around her petite body and draw her near. I take my right hand, use my pointer finger and pull her chin up so she can see me. I lean in half way, waiting for her to make her move. She does. She stands up on her tiptoes and leans in. Our lips touch, A rapid fire flashes through my body all the way to my toes. Her tongue peeks at the edge of my lips, and I open for her. I suck her tongue inside my mouth, and she moans. Her arms wrap around my waist, and her nails cling to my sides. The kiss grows more intense. I moan and tighten my grip, pulling her closer to my body.

"Excuse me," a little voice says, breaking the fog in my brain from the hot kiss.

I feel a hand tugging at my lower jeans. I look

down and see a little boy dressed in a yellow and black checkered shirt, which says Champs soccer on the front.

"Hey there, buddy. Are you lost?" I ask.

"Umm. I need my ball back, sir," he says, pointing down between Sophia and me.

I look down where he points and see the black and white checkered ball that sits still between Sophia's feet. I bend down, grab it, and place it in his little hands. His eyes light up, and he smiles so big that on both sides of his mouth dimples appear.

"Thank you, sir." He runs off back to the field.

"Sophia, let's sit and talk." I reach for her hand. She takes it.

I direct us to the swing around the pond. The only people around are the ones jogging. Taking a seat, a nice breeze blows by, sending goose bumps on Sophia's arms. I place my arm around her to give her some warmth.

"Are you warm enough?" I ask.

"Yes," she says, shifting her body so we are facing one another.

"Linkin, I don't know how to say this." Sophia looks up at me. "I love you."

"I've missed you so much, Sophia. Every time I saw your name appear on my phone, it took all I had not to hit the talk button. I was upset with you but mostly upset with myself. I had to do some thinking and praying," I say.

For the first time, I tear up for what I'm about to say. I take a deep breath, in and out. The tightness in my chest lets up, and I place my hands on her face so I can see those beautiful brown eyes.

"You stole my heart the first day I saw you at the hospital. I watched you lay in that bed, so pale, and I was angry. As a man of God, I only needed prayed over you, but I wanted that guy to pay for what he did. God doesn't like ugly, but I think he brought me to you so we can save one another. I had a client who killed herself, and I couldn't help her, and since then, I have struggled. I got a call from your mother, and my heart ached for you. I think, that day, you stole my heart in the hospital room, and I have been yours since," I say, and I feel something wet fall down my face.

Sophia's hand comes up and wipes the wetness off my face. I have not cried in years. It's not sad tears that fall; it's happiness. She kisses me, feeding my body the desire I have been craving. Her lips are so soft and warm as they combine with mine.

I pull away, and her lips are red and swollen. "I love you, beautiful," I whisper and place my lips back to hers for savoring.

EPILOGUE

Sophia

One year later...

I WAKE UP and roll over to see my husband lying flat on his stomach with his hands under the pillow. His eyes are closed, and his hair is spiked all over the place. I giggle. He has been so patient with me. We still have not sealed the deal with sex. I'm still not ready. But we did get freaky under the sheets with exploring each other's bodies. I can just say he knows what to do with those big hands.

We decided to settle in Fort Mill, SC, and start a new life here. The three-bedroom house is located in the downtown area. The backyard is fenced-in; the patio spreads out like a half-moon shape that is made of red bricks. I've added two white rocking chairs and an end table in between. This is where I spend most of my time, reading and watching Linkin plant along the fence in the backyard.

The bed shifts.

"Hey, beautiful, come give me some sugar," he says, dragging me to him. His large body engulfs me in. His large arms wrap around me, and he places his chin on my head. "How did Mrs. Garland sleep last night?"

I swirled my finger around his chisel chest. "I slept good." I reach my hand around his neck and pull him in for a kiss. "I love you, my sexy husband."

He wiggles his eyebrows up and down. He shifts his body on top of mine, placing small kisses down my neck to my collar bone. I shiver. As he starts down my chest, he reaches for one of my breasts. His tongue swirls around my nipple, making moisture pool in my panties. With his tongue, he makes a path down the center of my body to the edge of my hair line. While I moan, he rubs my lips up and down with his finger. He places his mouth there, kissing through my panties, his hot breath sending butterflies to my stomach. I close my eyes and let my body just enjoy.

Just then, the phone rings. We both jump apart. The ringing is coming from Linkin's phone. He rolls over and grabs it.

"Malcom, it's eight a.m. What is so important to be calling…" He stiffens up. "Okay, man, calm down. I am on my way," he says, hanging up. His back is to me, but I can tell from his breathing that something's wrong.

"Linkin, what's wrong?"

He shakes his head and stands up. "Darcy fell down the stairs and is having severe pain in her abdomen. Malcom says she's bleeding really bad. He called 911."

Oh, God.

I jump up and dig some clothes out of the dresser. I walk over to him and place my hand on his back. "Hey, she will be okay. Just because you had a dream that she died does not mean anything," I say, rubbing his back.

He woke up one night, screaming out Darcy's name. His body was covered in sweat. He's been having several dreams about her dying, and it's worrying him.

He lowers himself to the ground on his knees, and I follow as he prays out loud for God to watch over Darcy.

He grabs my hand and squeezes it tight. "I love you."

ACKNOWLEDGMENTS

I want to thank everyone who has read and corrected my paper. Each person has truly been very helpful.

I cannot express enough thanks to my editor, Monica Bogza, of Trusted Accomplice. I was given her information from another author to help me on my new journey of becoming a writer. I am grateful for her friendship, advice, and late nights where we talk about my books. Thank you for your dedication and hard work.

To my family, who has supported me in this decision to start writing. I work a full-time job then come home and write until bed time. My husband and kids have shown so much support; they even sit on the couch with me while I type.

To Bella Management Media for the premade cover for my book. I am amazed at the perfect result.

Thank you Kathy Grobusky, Toni Clinton, and Marie Mcmanus for the countless hours of reading and for encouraging me. Thank you to my mother in-law, Jackie Rivers, who took time also to read and pushed me to start the second book because she had to know about the other characters.

To all my author friends who took time out of

their work to help me with mine. You all welcomed me with open arms, and I am so thankful.

To all my readers who enjoy this book.

ALSO BY LYNN HAMMOND

In publication order

Alaskan Love Voyage

Loving Lies Series
Risky Lies
Bloom

The Chaplain Series
Surrender for Love – *Coming soon* (Darcy's story)
Discovering Love Again – *Coming soon*
(Malcom's story)

ABOUT LYNN HAMMOND

Lynn Hammond works full-time as a LPN but writes at night. She lives in Rock Hill, South Carolina. She is a RWA member. She loves to make children's tutus in her spare time. Every night before bed, she takes time to read. She loves romance, paranormal romance, and erotica. She is a proud mother of three beautiful girls, two beautiful grandbabies, two boxer pups, two lizards, four ducks, and loves spending time with her husband, riding in her father's old corvette. She is a new author, writing New Adult romance and would love to hear from readers.

You can contact her at
lynnhammondauthor@gmail.com.
Or come say hi on her Facebook page at:
facebook.com/lynn.hammond.10888

9 780692 132944